THE PUPPY RESCUE Girl Scout MYSTERY

by Carole Marsh

First Edition ©2018 Carole Marsh/Gallopade International/Peachtree City, GA
Current Edition © February 2018
Ebook edition ©2018
All rights reserved.
Manufactured in Peachtree City, GA

Published by Gallopade International/Carole Marsh Books. Printed in the United States of America.

This book is not authorized, approved, licensed, or endorsed by Girl Scouts of the USA. The GIRL SCOUT name, mark, and all associated trademarks and logotypes are owned by Girl Scouts of the USA.

Managing Editor: Janice Baker
Assistant Editor: Susan Walworth
Cover Design: John Hanson
Content Design: John Hanson

Gallopade is proud to be a member and supporter of these educational organizations and associations:

American Booksellers Association
American Library Association
International Reading Association
National Association for Gifted Children
The National School Supply and Equipment Association
The National Council for the Social Studies
Museum Store Association
Public Lands Alliance
Association of Booksellers for Children
Association for the Study of African American Life and History
National Alliance of Black School Educators

This book is a complete work of fiction. All events are fictionalized, and although the names of real people are used, their characterization in this book is fiction. All attractions, product names, or other works mentioned in this book are trademarks of their respective owners, and the names and images used in this book are strictly for editorial purposes; no commercial claims to their use is claimed by the author or publisher.

Dear Readers,

I'm so excited about this mystery about RESCUE PUPS! My rescue pup is named Coconut. An agency called Noah's Ark found her wandering the streets of Charleston, South Carolina. She weighed about four pounds and was around four months old. Noah's  Ark and a local veterinarian took good care of her. Soon, she turned up at a local dog rescue place (via the back door), just as I was coming in the front door.

"I am looking for a small white dog to rescue," I said. They replied, "We just had one come in; would you like to meet her?" Coconut came running up. She ran into my arms and stayed there.

It was like we were made for each other! We have been fast friends ever since.

I just wrote a book called *Tell Me Again About How You Rescued Me!* You might find it in your school library, local library, or a bookstore. You can also order a custom book with your own dog on the cover!

I hope you enjoy this book as you learn more about rescuing dogs that need a Forever Home!

Happy Scouting!

Carole Marsh

Carole Marsh and Coconut, her rescue pup

TABLE OF CONTENTS

1 Coconut Commotion..9
2 Doggie Fruit Salad..15
3 Who Let the Scouts Out?..21
4 One Good Turn...31
5 In the Dog House 37
6 Hot-Diggety-Dog! 43
7 Peeping Scouts 51
8 Broadway Betty...55
9 Love at First Bark 63
10 Oscar the Rat..69
11 Sniffs and Scents 75
12 A Blue Clue...83
13 Time to Hunker 87
14 Chocolate Broccoli..93
15 Bony Fingers 103
16 Turn Around, Don't Drown 107
17 Puppy Rescue 115
18 Runaway Rescue 121
19 Puppies, Puppies Everywhere! 129
20 A Good Wind...135
   Talk About It!..144
   Bring It to Life!...146
   Scavenger Hunt 148
   SAT Glossary 149

8

1

COCONUT COMMOTION

Ella tugged on the leash like an elephant was on the other end. "Come on, Coconut," she pleaded. "You will love this!"

The little white dog dug her front claws into the sod and pulled back until her haunches were planted stubbornly on the ground.

Ella took one hand off the leash to quickly wipe her long brown hair from her sweaty face, then she resumed her game of tug-o-war. "It's your spa day," she said with a huff. "And I have bows for you!"

Ella's sister Avery peeked over an easel perched nearby in the yard. "Please keep it down!" she yelled. "Can't you see I'm working on an important project?"

"Well, my project is important too!" Ella yelled back. "Girl Scouts are supposed to do a good turn daily. And I'm really trying to do a good turn, if only Coconut would cooperate."

"You don't understand," Avery said firmly. "I'm trying to earn my Outdoor Art Explorer badge!"

"Just because you're a Junior Girl Scout and I'm a Brownie doesn't mean that what you do is more important than what I do," Ella replied.

"Yes, but sometimes you act like a half-baked Brownie," Avery said. "You know that Mimi's dog has a stubborn streak wider than Texas. Sometimes she acts more like a nut than a coconut!"

"But Mimi said if I get Coconut all spit and polished," Ella explained, "it could help me earn a Brownie pet badge and show everyone that I have what it takes to finally get a dog of my own!"

Avery laughed. "Well, you'd better start spittin' because that's the only way you're ever going to get her wet when she doesn't want to be wet!"

Exasperated, Ella dropped Coconut's leash. "Why are you so stubborn?" she fussed at the little dog. Coconut looked up at her with suspicious eyes. Ella then rolled up her jeans and stepped into the kiddie pool that Mimi had bought when the girls were toddlers. The bright blue pool was decorated with pictures of smiling dolphins jumping through multicolored rings.

Ella had filled the pool with water early that morning so the sun could warm it. She stood still until the surface was as smooth as a mirror. She could see her reflection and the fluffy cumulus clouds floating by in an aqua sky. It reminded her of her Brownie Investiture Ceremony where she learned the legend of the little elves called Brownies that sneak into homes and do chores. Ella still remembered the rhyme she had to say: "Twist me, and turn me and show me the elf, I looked in the mirror and saw myself."

Glancing at Coconut, Ella said, "Look how fun this is!" She squeezed a generous dollop of dog shampoo into the water and swished it with her feet until a lather of creamy bubbles covered the surface.

Coconut watched Ella curiously and crept closer to see the bubbles escaping into the air.

Avery and Ella's younger sister Sadie, a Daisy Scout, was playing with her dolls on the back porch. "Something smells like coconut!" she shouted suddenly.

"I bought some coconut-scented dog shampoo," Ella replied. "I figured a dog named Coconut should smell like a coconut!"

"It smells like Mimi's Christmas cakes and one of my favorite Girl Scout cookies," Sadie said.

Avery, who had also caught a whiff of the coconut scent, added, "Too bad it's not cookie-selling time. I can almost taste that caramel and coconut cookie drizzled with chocolate! Yum!"

Ella nodded in agreement, acting totally disinterested in Coconut, whose nose was now over the pool. Finally seeing her opportunity, Ella lunged for the leash. She pulled Coconut into the frothy water before the little dog realized what was happening.

Coconut froze. A glob of soapsuds stood on her head like whipped cream on an ice-cream sundae. But once she realized she was standing in water, she yelped and shot straight into the air like she had springs for legs. For several steps she seemed to walk on water before her feet were back on the grass. Then Coconut tore straight toward Avery's easel with the bright pink leash flapping behind her like a kite's tail.

"Coconut, NO!" Avery shouted. The **cantankerous** canine knocked a leg out from under the easel, bringing a rainbow of paint tumbling down onto her back.

"Please stop, Coco!" Ella hollered as she chased after the puppy. But stopping was the last thing on Coconut's mind. She shot toward Mimi's back door like a multicolored missile. Ella saw her grandmother crack the door to see what all the commotion was about.

"Mimi!" Ella shouted. "Don't open the door!" But it was too late. Coconut rocketed onto the back porch and knocked a doll out of Sadie's hand. The dog then raced into the house, where she launched onto Mimi's white couch.

Mimi stood with her mouth open in shock, her sparkly red reading glasses balanced near the end of her nose. She looked at the colorful dog on her couch and back at Ella, who had chased her inside. Coconut stared at them both with an expression of dog laughter. Every wag of her fluffy tail splattered a new pattern on the back of the sofa like an artist's brush.

Sadie burst through the door in tears. "My baby doll has a tattoo!" she wailed and pointed to the colorful smear that Coconut had brushed across the doll's cheek. Avery marched behind Sadie, her painting in hand. The tree she had painted now had multicolor paw prints marching across the center. "My painting is ruined!" she cried.

"My new couch," Mimi moaned, holding her chin in her hands.

Ella sighed. "Now I'll never get my pet care badge or a dog of my own!"

2

DOGGIE FRUIT SALAD

After two shampoos in Mimi's bathtub, the rainbow colors swirled through Coconut's coat looked like a faded lollipop. "Guess I'll have a painted puppy for a while," Mimi observed.

"And a colorful couch," Avery added.

"Thanks for reminding me," Mimi mumbled. She glanced over at her comfy couch, not sure whether to laugh or cry.

"I'm so sorry, Mimi," Ella said, wrapping her arms around her grandmother. "I thought I was doing you a favor by bathing Coconut. But all I did was mess up everything. I was so excited about staying with you while Mom and Dad are out of town. After all this, you'll probably never want us to stay with you again!"

Mimi's expression softened. "Hogwash!" she said. "You are always welcome at Mimi's house. Your antics keep me young and vibrant!" Mimi pursed her lips, put one hand on her hip, and fluffed her short blonde hair like a movie star. The girls giggled.

"You didn't do any of this on purpose," Mimi told Ella. "Coconut can be extremely stubborn. But her occasional stubbornness is nothing compared to everything she gives me."

"Lots of headaches?" Avery asked.

Mimi chuckled and whistled to Coconut. The fluffy pup leaped into her arms. As Mimi cradled the little dog and gently rubbed her head, she said, "Coconut's life started out rough. She was found in the streets when she was a tiny puppy. She wasn't wearing a collar. No one's sure if she was dumped or if she got lost. She had seizures and a local vet was kind enough to take her in and treat her until she was strong enough to be adopted.

"When I showed up at the rescue organization that was trying to find Coconut a permanent home," Mimi continued, "I told them I was looking for a *small* rescue dog. I certainly wasn't looking for a puppy! But when they brought Coconut out—all four pounds of her—she was sooooo cute and loving! Our eyes met, and I knew she'd be mine forever. Honestly, we rescued each other! Since then she's been my sweet, sweet, sweet little pomegranate!"

"Wait a minute, Mimi," Ella said. "You've got your fruits mixed up! You called her a pomegranate instead of a coconut."

"She was already named Coconut when I adopted her," Mimi explained. "I call her a pomegranate because her DNA test showed that she is part Pomeranian, part Maltese, part Cocker Spaniel, and part Chihuahua!"

"Wow!" Ella said. "She's like a doggie fruit salad!"

"And now she even looks like a fruit salad!" Sadie added, running her fingers through the red, yellow, orange and blue streaks in Coconut's fur.

"Is adopting Coconut what made you want to write a book about rescue dogs?" Ella asked. Mimi, a famous writer of books for children, couldn't pass up the chance to write about one of her newest passions: rescue dogs.

"You hit it right on the warm, wet, doggie nose!" Mimi said. "Even though I'm known for all my mystery books, I want kids to learn about these special dogs who need homes."

"Are there a lot of homeless dogs?" Avery asked.

"Sadly, yes," Mimi answered. "There are a lot of homeless dogs all over the country—and the world." She kissed Coconut's colorful head and placed her gently on the floor. "Why don't you girls get everything picked up in the backyard. Your Girl Scout meeting starts in an hour. I want to check the weather and see what the hurricane's up to."

"Hurricane?" Ella asked. "What hurricane? The weather's beautiful!"

"Hurricane Kevin," Mimi replied. "It's still far out in the ocean, but some of the meteorologists predict it could come our way. I want to keep an eye on it."

"Let's hope Kevin doesn't keep his 'eye' on us!" Avery said.

"What??" Ella asked, confused.

"Hurricanes have an eye," Avery explained. "It's the center of the storm."

"If a hurricane only has one eye, it should be called a 'cyclops' instead," Ella said. "You know—the giants with only one eye in the center of their head."

Avery threw her hands up in exasperation and pushed open the back door. "I know what a cyclops is," she said. "You'll learn more about hurricanes when you're older."

Outside, Avery picked up her paints and easel while Ella decided to empty the coconut-scented water from the kiddie pool.

Ella looked around the yard and scratched her head. "Did you already move the kiddie pool?" she asked her sister.

"No," Avery answered. "I've been with you the whole time."

"Then where is it?" Ella asked, spinning to view the entire yard. "It's disappeared into thin air!"

"That's weird," Avery said, joining Ella where the pool had been.

Ella stomped the ground and water splashed onto her shoes. Then she sniffed the air. "Well, the water's still here," she observed. "And the grass smells like coconut. Any chance some early hurricane winds blew the empty pool away?"

Avery licked her finger and held it up. "The hurricane's still very far away," she said. "There's not much wind at all."

"Well, now we have one big mystery on our hands!" Ella exclaimed, frowning. Then she remembered the little elves called Brownies she'd thought of while standing in the pool.

Did Brownies come and take the pool away? she wondered.

20

3

WHO LET THE SCOUTS OUT?

During the drive to the Girl Scout meeting, Ella stared out the window at the tall pines standing at attention beside the road. Soon they gave way to a tunnel of live oaks with thick trunks. Wisps of Spanish moss hung from their twisted limbs. Ella liked to call them "witches' wigs."

When they exited the tunnel of trees, Ella glimpsed the marshland in the distance. The slanting last rays of sun glowed on patches of water like glistening fire. She also noticed a strange-looking house standing alone on a hill overlooking the marsh. Ella thought it was a dead ringer for a house she had seen in a scary movie. Except for two lights glowing from first-floor windows, it was dark. Although she loved the beautiful scenery of the Lowcountry, including the marsh, Ella shuddered at the thought of living in such a place.

When she could no longer see the spooky house, thoughts of the missing kiddie pool returned to slosh through Ella's mind. Mimi had assured them she knew nothing of the pool's whereabouts. "I don't like to let the pool stay on the grass for very long," she had said. "It leaves a big yellow circle on my lawn. But I was much too busy bathing a painted dog to move it!"

Avery glanced at her sister. Sensing that Ella was thinking about the missing pool, Avery said, "Someone must have taken the pool while we were inside."

"Who could possibly want that old thing?" Ella asked. "It's cheap plastic. Besides, swimming season is over."

Mimi overheard their conversation. "Maybe that's what Coconut was trying to tell you," she said with a chuckle. "Stop worrying about the kiddie pool, girls. If it doesn't turn up, I'll get you another one to splash in next spring."

"Yes, baby Ella will need her baby pool to splash in," Avery said in a baby voice.

Ella's face grew red. "I'm a better swimmer than you are!" she shot back. "I just like to cool off in the pool. Plus, Sadie likes it too!"

"I like the pool," Sadie added. "My dolls like to swim in it with me!"

"Now, girls," Mimi scolded, as she pulled into the community center parking lot to drop off the girls for their Girl Scout meeting. "You've forgotten your promise to live by the Girl Scout Law! Doesn't it say something about getting along?"

"Well, yes, it kind of does..." Avery mumbled.

"Hmmm," Mimi hummed and tapped her chin. "Is it considerate and caring to call your sister a baby? And Ella, is it friendly and helpful to boast that you're a better swimmer? Remember, you have to be a sister to every Girl Scout, even if she's your real sister."

"You're right," Avery said, glancing sideways at Ella.

"Sorry, Mimi," Ella apologized.

"Have fun at your meeting," Mimi said. "Now, skedaddle. I'm going shopping for something to make Coconut and my couch white again!"

Inside, the girls' troop leaders steered everyone into one room. "Brownies, Juniors, and Daisies are meeting together tonight," Mrs. Brown explained. She was Avery's troop leader.

"Great," Avery muttered under her breath. Then, remembering Mimi's reminder about the Girl Scout Law, Avery looked at Ella and forced a smile.

"We've got a special surprise," Mrs. Brown said. "You're going to love it!"

Ella remembered telling Coconut the same thing when she tried to get her into the kiddie pool. She hoped this surprise turned out better than Coconut's.

Inside the meeting hall, Sadie joined her Daisy leader and a group of Daisies in one corner. Avery's friend Aniyah—a tall, willowy girl who liked to wear a bun on top of her head—waved her over to a huddled group of Juniors. Left alone, Ella noticed a girl that she'd never seen. The girl twisted her Brownie beanie nervously in her hands and stared shyly at her shoes.

"Mind if I sit with you?" Ella asked. "My name is Ella."

The girl nodded. "I'm Laila," she said.

"Are you new here?" Ella asked.

"We just moved here about a week ago," she answered. "My grandmother made me come to this meeting."

"Well, my grandmother brought me to the meeting too," Ella chatted on. "But I wanted to come! I love being a Brownie! Weren't you a Brownie before you moved here?"

"You don't understand," Laila answered sadly. But before she could say more, the troop leaders called the meeting to order.

After everyone recited the Pledge of Allegiance, Mrs. Brown asked the girls to recite the Girl Scout Promise. Laila glanced around with a panicked expression. "I don't know it," she whispered to Ella.

Ella quickly showed her how to hold up three fingers on her right hand to represent the three promises. "I'll teach you the words later," she said before reciting the promise with the other girls.

Mrs. Brown then asked all the girls—Brownies, Juniors, and Daisies—to stand in a circle. She held up a balloon and said, "When the music begins, try to keep the balloon in the air. If you're touching the balloon when the music stops, you have to pop it and do what the message inside tells you to do."

As the tune of "You Ain't Nothin' But a Hound Dog," blared from speakers, Mrs. Brown changed the lyrics to "You Ain't Nothin' But a Girl Scout." The girls giggled and sang and bopped the green balloon around the circle. Avery was the last person to touch it when the music stopped. "How can I pop it?" she asked Mrs. Brown. "I don't have a pin."

"Sit on it," Mrs. Brown suggested.

The girls roared with laughter as Avery sat on the balloon and wiggled furiously until it popped beneath her. She picked up the note that had been inside the balloon and read it silently. "You've got to be kidding," she said, her flushing cheeks signaling that she was embarrassed by what the note told her to do.

"Come on, Avery!" Mrs. Brown said. "Be a good sport or the game's no fun."

Hesitantly, Avery got on all fours, turned her head to one side and started turning in circles.

"Can anyone guess what she's doing?" Mrs. Brown asked.

"She's looking for a lost earring!" one girl suggested. The girls giggled.

"No, that's not it," Mrs. Brown said.

"She looks like my dog when he chases his tail," another girl offered.

"You're right!" Mrs. Brown said excitedly, before starting the music again. Avery stood up, relieved that her dog impersonation was over. This time, the tune was "Who Let the Dogs Out," but the girls immediately started singing, "Who Let the Scouts Out—woof, woof, woof, woof!"

When the music stopped again, a Brownie named Clara was holding the balloon. She popped it with her foot. When she read her note, she looked at the ceiling and started howling.

"She's howling at the moon!" Ella shouted.

"You got it!" Mrs. Brown said.

After several more rounds, it was apparent that every note inside the balloons required the girls to imitate something dogs do.

Once all the balloons were popped, Mrs. Brown explained, "We played this game to give you a hint about a special community service project. Brownies and Juniors will work together to help our local animal shelter with dogs that need homes. This project will give you the opportunity to earn the pet care badge."

Ella made a fist in the air and pulled it down swiftly. "Yesss!" she said. "That's the one I wanted to earn! Now, I won't have to depend on Coconut to help me!" She turned to give Laila a high five. But to her surprise, Laila was no longer beside her. Ella surveyed the circle of girls, but her new acquaintance had disappeared.

4

ONE GOOD TURN

The girls piled into Mimi's car when she arrived to pick them up. But as soon as she rounded the corner of the building, Ella yelled "STOP!"

"What did you forget *this* time?" Avery asked, a bit annoyed.

"Nothing," Ella answered, "but I have to get out of the car. I'll be back in two shakes of a lamb's tail!"

Mimi was puzzled, but she pulled into a parking space. Ella jumped out of the car and slammed the door behind her. She had spotted Laila sitting on a bench under a lamp post. Tears glistened on her cheeks. "Are you OK?" Ella asked. "When you disappeared

31

from the meeting, I didn't know what had happened to you."

"I'll be OK," Laila answered. "I called my grandmother to pick me up. It was too hard in there."

"Too hard?" Ella questioned. "Because you don't know the Girl Scout Promise? I promise I'll teach you."

"It's not that," Laila said. "It was all the talk about dogs."

"Oh, I get it," Ella said. "You don't like dogs. After what I went through with my grandmother's dog this afternoon, that's understandable."

"No!" Laila exclaimed. "I love dogs!"

"Then what's the problem?" Ella was puzzled.

"When my mother and I moved here to live with my grandmother," Laila explained, "I had to leave my dog behind in Chicago." New tears streamed from Laila's eyes. "His name is Tucker. He was my best friend. We adopted him from an animal shelter when he was a puppy and we were the only family he'd ever known."

"But why couldn't you bring him?" Ella asked.

"It was too expensive to bring him on the airplane, and my grandmother doesn't like dogs," Laila explained. "A dog bit her when she was a little girl, so she's been afraid of dogs ever since. But Tucker never bit anyone. He was the sweetest dog in the world. And he was smart. I taught him to shake, roll over, and speak."

"How sad," Ella said, tears welling in her own eyes. "Where is Tucker now?"

"We had to return him to the shelter where we adopted him," Laila said. "It was the worst day of my life. Now I'm worried he'll wind up going home with someone who won't love him as much as I did."

"I'm so sorry," Ella said. "Would you like to come over tomorrow and play with my grandmother's dog, Coconut? She's very stubborn, but she's also very sweet. Maybe you can help me teach her some tricks!"

"That would be great!" Laila said, her expression brightening.

When a car pulled into the parking space beside Mimi's car, Laila said, "That's my grandmother."

"Great!" Ella said. "Our grandmothers can exchange phone numbers."

"What took you so long?" Avery asked impatiently when Ella climbed back into Mimi's car.

"That was more like 10,000 shakes of a lamb's tail instead of two," Sadie added.

"It takes time to solve a mystery," Ella explained.

"You mean you found out what happened to the kiddie pool?" Avery asked.

"No," Ella replied. "But I found out why my new friend is sad, and I helped her feel better. Not to brag, but I followed the Girl Scout Law. I was friendly, helpful, considerate, and caring. And since my good turn of bathing Coconut was such a disaster, I'm also counting it as my good turn for today."

Avery gave Ella a high-five. "I'm good with that," she said. "And at least you solved one mystery. One down, with two to go."

"What do you mean by 'two'?" Ella asked. "What mystery is there other than the missing pool?"

"The animal shelter where we're supposed to volunteer," Avery said.

"What about it?" Ella asked.

Avery replied, "We just heard on the radio that some of the dogs there have mysteriously disappeared!"

5

IN THE DOG HOUSE

The next morning, Avery called Mrs. Brown to see if their project was still on after the upsetting news about the missing dogs. "It hasn't been canceled," Avery said when she hung up. "She said there are still plenty of animals to help at the shelter."

"Does Mrs. Brown know what happened to the dogs?" Ella asked.

"No," Avery replied. "It's bizarre. Maybe we'll learn more when we go to the shelter."

After breakfast, Mimi took Avery, Ella, and Sadie to a fabric store. The girls needed to buy material for dog blankets they wanted to make and donate to the animal shelter as part of their pet project.

Sadie quickly chose a pink piece of fleece with snowflakes on it. Then she joined Mimi to look for upholstery fabric. "If I can't get the paint off my couch, maybe I can make a new cover for it," Mimi murmured.

Ella found a piece of blue fleece with yellow bones printed on it that she thought was perfect for her blanket.

"I like this one!" Avery exclaimed, rubbing her fingers along a section of purple fake-fur material. "It's so soft! And the puppies would think it's their mother!"

"I've never seen a puppy with a purple mother!" Ella said, laughing.

"They wouldn't know it's purple," Avery said. "Don't you know that dogs are color blind?"

"That's not true!" Ella protested. "I read that dogs can't see as many colors as humans, but they can see some colors—mostly blues, yellows and shades of gray. That's why I chose blue and yellow material."

"That's so sad!" Avery said. "Dogs miss out on so many beautiful things! And poor

Coconut can't even see all the beautiful colors she painted on Mimi's couch!"

"Don't worry," Ella said. "Dogs may not see all colors, but they are super sniffers! My book said that a dog's sense of smell is 10,000 to 100,000 times better than a human's sense of smell." She held the fake fur to her nose and sneezed. "Avery, this is NOT the fabric for a dog's sensitive nose. It smells awful!"

"OK, you win," Avery said. "No purple fur." She rummaged through a huge cardboard bin filled with fabric **remnants**. She spied a yellow piece of fleece with black and white soccer balls on it. "How's this one?" she asked.

"Perfect!" Ella replied with a thumbs up sign.

But when Avery started to pull the material out of the bin, it wouldn't budge. "Must be hung on something," she said, giving it a yank.

Ella had walked around the bin to help her sister when she heard a familiar voice complaining, "Ugggh! It's stuck!" She fell against the bin laughing. Her new friend Laila was tugging on the same piece of fabric that Avery was pulling from the opposite side!

"Let me help you," Ella whispered to Laila and snickered mischievously. She grabbed the fabric and leaned back with all her might. In a second, Avery let out a yelp as she was pulled head first into the mountain of material! When she stood up, a bright blue piece of fake fur covered her blonde hair like a clown wig.

"Now, any dog could see that hair!" Ella exclaimed.

"I'm not sure that they would want to!" Laila added, giggling.

"Very funny," Avery grumbled. "Now get me out of here before we're all in the doghouse. Mimi will be so embarrassed if she sees us, and that store clerk over there doesn't look amused."

The girls helped Avery out of the fabric bin. Holding the piece of fabric she had won in the tug-of-war, Laila said, "There's plenty of this fabric to make several dog blankets. We can share."

"Great idea!" Ella said as Laila's grandmother walked up with Mimi and Sadie.

"What's a great idea?" Mimi asked.

"Mimi, Laila and I had already planned for Laila to come over," Ella replied. "She could come today, and we can all work together to make the blankets!"

Laila looked at her grandmother for approval. "You can go," she said, "if Ella's grandmother doesn't mind."

When the girls took their fabric to the register, the clerk peered at them curiously. They expected a scolding for playing in the fabric bin. Instead, the woman asked, "Why is everyone making blankets today?"

"We're doing a Girl Scout project," Avery explained.

"I just rang up fabric for an elderly lady," the clerk said. "She was making blankets too, but I don't know if they were for dogs. It was yellow fleece with blue fire hydrants on it—something I imagine dogs would like." The clerk pointed toward the door where a gray-haired woman was pulling a hood over her head before going out. "Of course," the clerk added with a laugh, "she's too old to be a Girl Scout!"

While Mimi paid for the fabric, Ella noticed a bright pink slip of paper on the floor near the register. It looked like it was torn from a small notepad like the one Mimi always used for her shopping lists. On the bottom was a printed outline of a dog encircled with a heart. Ella picked up the paper to toss it into a nearby trash can. But she stopped when she noticed that it was a list of pet supplies with checkmarks next to each item. The last item on the list was fabric.

She wasn't sure why, but something about the list struck Ella as odd. "Hmmm," she pondered. "This must have been that lady's list, and maybe her fabric *was* for dog blankets!"

6

HOT-DIGGETY-DOG!

Back at Mimi's house, the girls helped make mini corn dogs and French fries for lunch.

Shortly after they popped the corn dogs into the oven, Avery said, "They smell delicious! I love corn dogs!"

"Me too!" Sadie exclaimed while jumping into the air like a cheerleader.

"They're not corn dogs," Ella said. "They're hot-diggity-dogs!"

"What?" Avery asked.

"Yes!" Ella said. "As soon as you taste them, you'll say, "Hot-Diggity-Dog!"

Mimi laughed. "It's the perfect food for a dog blanket-making party! After all, the shelter dogs won't be 'chili dogs' after they get their blankets. They'll be 'hot dogs'!"

"Oh, Mimi," Avery groaned. "That joke was cornier than the corn dogs!"

While they waited for the corn dogs to bake, the girls and Mimi watched the latest weather forecast for Hurricane Kevin on television.

"What are all those lines for?" Ella asked when the meteorologist brought up a map of the eastern United States with squiggly lines in the Atlantic Ocean.

"Those are the possible paths that Kevin could take," Mimi answered with a concerned look. "Meteorologists never know for certain what a hurricane will do. They take what they know and make an educated guess." She traced one of the lines on the TV. "But that blue line right there has Kevin knocking on our door."

"Don't worry, Mimi," Sadie said. "I won't answer the door."

Mimi smiled and hugged her littlest granddaughter. "I wish it were that easy," she said. "Unfortunately, visits from hurricanes are a part of life when you live near the coast."

Aniyah and Laila arrived as Mimi pulled the corn dogs from the oven. "Hot-diggity-dog!" Aniyah exclaimed. "My favorite!"

"Told you!" Ella said, nodding her head confidently at Avery.

After lunch, the girls went to Mimi's back porch to make blankets while Sadie stayed inside to make her blanket with Mimi. Avery had borrowed Mimi's measuring tape and draped it around her neck. "Each blanket is supposed to use one yard of fabric," she instructed.

Once Avery and Aniyah had cut all the fabric into rectangles, the girls cut slits all the way around each piece to make fringe. Then they knotted each piece of fringe.

Curious, Coconut sniffed the blanket Ella was working on. She suddenly grabbed it with her tiny teeth and pulled. "Hey, stop it," Ella yelled. "This blanket isn't for you!"

Still looking like a furry rainbow, Coconut stared at Ella like a defiant kindergartner.

"Ugggh!" Ella groaned.

Laila slipped into the house and quickly returned with something in her hand.

"Coconut, come!" she commanded.

Coconut dropped the blanket and obediently walked over to Laila. "Sit!" Laila commanded and raised her hand in front of Coconut's nose until she sat.

"Wow!" Ella said. "You're good! How'd you do that?"

Laila fed Coconut what was in her hand. "She likes corn dogs," she said. "When you train a dog, you start with treats and lead their nose with the treat. Watch this."

Laila took another piece of corn dog and guided Coconut's nose down until she was lying on the porch floor. "Down!" she commanded.

"That's awesome!" Ella exclaimed. "I wish I had known that when I was trying to get her into the pool!"

"What pool?" Aniyah asked.

Avery and Ella told their friends about the mysterious missing pool as well as the commotion with Coconut and the paint.

"How could a pool disappear into thin air?" Aniyah asked.

"Maybe aliens beamed it up into their spaceship?" Laila offered and grinned slyly.

Ella giggled. "Right," she said. "On some faraway planet, a little green kid is splashing in our kiddie pool."

"I've heard there are witches that live in the marshland around here," Aniyah said. "Maybe one of them needed it to make her witches' brew."

Ella thought of the creepy house she had seen on the edge of the marsh while they were driving to the Girl Scout meeting. *Does a witch live there?* She shivered.

Avery rolled her eyes. "It couldn't disappear into thin air," she asserted. "There's got to be some sort of clue. Maybe we should take one more look in the backyard. Aniyah and Laila might see something we missed."

Avery and Aniyah searched one side of the yard while Ella and Laila searched the area where the pool had been. Coconut curiously sniffed the circle of grass flattened by the pool.

"She smells something," Laila said.

"Of course," Ella answered. "She's always sniffing something."

"No," Laila said. "She's sniffed one spot for a while and now she's following the scent toward the gate. That's probably how the burglar, or little green men, or whoever, carried the pool out of here. Let's see where she leads us."

When Coconut stopped at the gate, Ella noticed a small scrap of paper.

"I found something!" she yelled to Avery and Aniyah. "It's a receipt for dog food."

Simply Pure milk	$2.99
Golden Farms eggs	$1.89
Crunchy Bones dog food	$9.99

"Maybe your Mimi dropped it," Laila suggested.

Ella frowned when she read the receipt. "Crunchy Bones...hmmm. That isn't the brand of dog food that Coconut eats," she announced.

7

PEEPING SCOUTS

Arf! Arf! Arf arf arf! Coconut barked in staccato bursts at something moving behind the board fence that divided Mimi's backyard from her neighbor's. The girls, still perplexed by the out-of-place dog food receipt, ran to see what had Coconut so upset. Each of them chose one of the narrow cracks between the boards and peered as best they could to the other side.

"I don't see our kiddie pool, but there's a dog over there!" Ella exclaimed in an animated whisper.

"A big one!" Laila agreed.

"Are you sure?" Avery asked. "I can't see much of anything." But seconds later she yelled, "Oh, yucky!! Ewwww!"

"What's wrong with you?" Ella asked.

"I finally saw the dog," Avery said, rubbing her eye. "He stuck his big wet nose right through the crack and into my eyeball—so disgusting!"

Ella and Laila covered their mouth with their hands to keep from laughing out loud.

"Oh! I see a boy," Aniyah announced. "His hair is red, and he's got something in his hand—a stick or something." Aniyah turned her body, trying to follow him with her one eye that was looking through the crack, but he was quickly out of view. The girls went from crack to crack trying to get another glimpse of the boy. Soon they heard a door slam.

"He went inside with the dog," Avery said.

"Before we were peeking through the fence at him, maybe he was peeking through the fence at us!" Aniyah speculated.

"That's right!" Ella said. "He probably watched the whole time I was trying to give Coconut a bath yesterday, and he knew when we went inside."

"Does your grandmother know him?" Aniyah asked.

"No, I don't think she's met those neighbors yet," Avery said. "She said they keep to themselves."

"Since they have a dog, maybe that's where the dog food receipt came from," Laila suggested.

"That's possible," Ella agreed. "Maybe the red-headed boy dropped it when he came to swipe our kiddie pool after he saw us go inside."

"Now wait a minute," Avery said. "You have no way of knowing that. You're accusing someone you haven't even met. Remember that as Girl Scouts we promise to be honest and fair. Since we don't have any proof that boy has anything to do with this, we shouldn't accuse him."

Ella nodded. "You're right," she said. She was still clutching the receipt in her hand. "Still, I'm keeping this receipt just in case I find out what kind of food that boy's dog eats. If it's Crunchy Bones, then this is a good piece of evidence." She smoothed the paper across her thigh so that she could fold it neatly. That was when she noticed the writing on the opposite side:

Friday 7:30 P.M.

8

BROADWAY BETTY

The next day, Avery, Ella, and Sadie met the other Girl Scouts at the T. Simmons Animal Shelter. A slim young man with thick brown hair pulled back in a ponytail welcomed them inside.

"I'm Eric," he said with a warm smile. "I'm the shelter manager, but one day I hope to be a veterinarian. I'm so glad you girls are here to help. And the blankets you made are awesome! They'll give our dogs that are waiting for 'furever' homes a cozy place to sleep. Much better than the cold, concrete floor."

Ella couldn't wait any longer to ask her question. "Did you find the animals that disappeared from the shelter?" she blurted out.

The grin slowly melted off Eric's face. "Oh," he said. "You heard about that. I'm afraid we haven't. It's a mystery."

Quickly changing the subject, Eric took a deep breath and continued, "Before you meet our furry residents, you need to learn some things about staying safe around animals. First, you should never approach or try to pet a strange dog that's not on a leash. That's asking for a dog bite. And dogs can carry diseases, including rabies. That goes for any kind of animal. Never approach or try to pick up any animal in the wild.

"If you meet a dog with its owner," Eric continued, "always ask the owner's permission to pet their dog. If the owner gives you permission, approach the dog from the side and gently pet it under the chin. Never approach a dog you don't know from the front. The dog could see that as a threat."

Eric waved his arm toward the hallway leading to the kennels. "Our dogs come from many different situations," he explained.

"Some are puppies. The most dangerous thing about them is their slobbery kisses."

The girls giggled. Ella whispered to Avery, "I can't wait to see them!"

"And some of our dogs were family pets that had to be surrendered to the shelter when their owners could no longer care for them," he added. "That's always a heartbreaking situation for the owner and the pet."

"That's terrible!" one girl exclaimed. "Why would someone ever put their pet in a shelter?"

Ella shot a quick glance at Laila, knowing that was the exact situation that happened with her dog Tucker. She saw the corners of her new friend's mouth quivering and could tell she was fighting back tears.

Eric continued. "Sometimes people move and can't take their pets with them, or sometimes elderly people have to move into a nursing home that doesn't accept pets. Sadly, some people adopt a cute puppy, but when it's an adult and no longer so cute or little, they decide they don't want it anymore. Many people don't realize the amount of work and expense involved in caring for pets.

"But the good news," he explained, "is that most of the dogs surrendered by their owners are safe to handle because they've been raised as family pets. That makes it easier to find new homes for them."

"What about dogs that are strays?" Avery asked.

"Some strays are family pets that have wandered away from home and become lost," Eric replied. "Of course, we also have strays that are feral animals."

"What are ferals?" Sadie asked. "Are they like hamsters?

Eric smiled at the question. "No," he said. "Feral animals are domesticated animals, like dogs or cats that normally live around humans. However, they are born without humans to care for them, so they have to live like wild animals. These animals are the most dangerous to work with and the most difficult to find homes for. But we work very hard to tame them and make them suitable to be pets."

"What happens to the animals you can't find homes for?" Aniyah asked.

"Fortunately," Eric said, "this animal shelter never puts animals to sleep."

"Why did we make blankets if the animals here never go to sleep?" a young Brownie asked.

"Being 'put to sleep' means being killed," Eric said. The young girl looked at Eric in horror.

"We work hard to find a home for every single animal we take in," Eric said. "We get help from lots of different rescue groups that have connections all over the country. For example, once we took in a little stray that looked like a mix between a poodle and a Chihuahua. She had been living in a storm drain. She was so caked with mud that it took three baths before we found out she had white curly fur with a black patch around her right eye. Her ears looked too big for her body and stood straight up." Eric held his fingers up on top of his head to demonstrate how her ears looked.

"But thanks to a rescue group," he explained, "she found a great home in New York City with an actress who lives in a fancy, high-rise apartment," Eric said. "She named her Betty and sent us a picture of her sleeping in a sparkly dog bed. Helping animals find great homes is the T. Simmons way."

"Who is T. Simmons?" Avery asked.

"It's actually Twila Simmons. She started this shelter," Eric replied. "She loved animals, especially dogs. She believed every dog deserved a great home."

"She sounds like the founder of the Girl Scouts, Juliette Gordon Low," Avery said. "Her nickname was Daisy and she loved animals too."

"That's right," Mrs. Brown said. "They recently unveiled a statue of Juliette and her dog at her birthplace in Savannah, Georgia."

"Will we get to meet Mrs. Simmons?" Ella asked.

"No," Eric said. "I'm not even sure she's still living. Years ago, Mrs. Simmons and the shelter's board of directors had a disagreement. They thought she was too old to work at the shelter."

"That doesn't seem fair," Ella said.

Eric shifted his feet uncomfortably and quickly changed the subject. "Now," he said, "who's ready to meet some puppies?"

All the girls raised their hands excitedly except Ella. She was trying to figure out why Eric seemed uncomfortable talking about Twila Simmons.

"There may be a lot of dogs here," Ella whispered to Avery. "But it wouldn't surprise me to find some sea creatures too."

"Sea creatures!?!?" Avery exclaimed, twisting her face into a look of confusion. "What are you talking about?"

"Something here is fishy," Ella said, narrowing her eyes in suspicion.

9

LOVE AT FIRST BARK

Under Eric's direction, the Girl Scouts quickly split up around the shelter, cleaning kennels, distributing the blankets they'd made, feeding and watering, and grooming dogs.

Ella soon forgot about Mrs. Simmons, Coconut, Mimi's stained couch, and everything else that was worrying her as soon as her eyes met one of the shelter residents.

"Awwwww!" Ella cried as Eric led a chubby yellow puppy toward her and Laila. "We named this guy Wyatt," Eric said. "I thought you two girls could give him and then his littermates a bath." The puppy sat and cocked his head to one side to look at them. "He's the sweetest little Labrador Retriever you'll ever meet,"

Eric said. "You'll find shampoo and towels in the office closet."

Ella circled to Wyatt's side as Eric had taught them. Then she gently scratched the pup under his chin. He wagged his tail shyly and looked at her with mournful brown eyes.

"He looks sad," Ella said. "Is he OK?"

"Wyatt and his littermates were found abandoned beside a dirt road," Eric replied. "That's why he's so dirty."

"He probably misses his mother," Laila said as she gently scratched his head and the silky-soft triangles that were his ears.

Wyatt gave each of the girls a grateful lick on the cheek and barked softly, "Whoof, whoof, whoof!"

"I think he is saying 'I love you,' to me," Ella commented. "I love you too, Wyatt! And when we get through with your makeover, you'll be adopted lickety-split."

"You'd better get started," Eric suggested. "You have a lot of puppy baths to give!"

The girls led Wyatt to a small utility room beside the shelter's office. While Laila adjusted the water temperature and tested it with her arm, Ella went into the office for the necessary supplies. She opened the closet door and pulled out a fluffy towel along with a huge bottle of dog shampoo.

"This is enough shampoo to bathe a whole pack of dogs," she muttered. Struggling to hold everything while closing the closet door, Ella knocked a stack of papers off a desk.

"Uggh!" she grumbled at her own clumsiness. She placed the supplies on the floor to pick up the scattered papers. After making a pancake stack, she tapped it to straighten the edges. That's when she noticed a small slip of paper slide onto the floor. It was a receipt for dog food. Ella noticed the dog food brand on the receipt–Crunchy Bones.

Ella told Laila about the receipt as they lathered Wyatt in the puppy tub. "I'm sure a lot of people use that brand of dog food," Laila said. Wyatt's eyes closed as he enjoyed the girls' fingers massaging his coat with the foamy shampoo.

"I guess you're right," Ella said. "It just seems odd. Call it my sixth sense or my mysterious nose."

Laila stared at Ella's nose. "It just looks like a plain old regular nose to me," she said.

Ella giggled. "I didn't mean that I have a mysterious nose. I meant to say that I have a nose for mystery. I probably inherited it from my Mimi who has spent most of her life writing mysteries."

"All I smell right now is a wet, stinky puppy," Laila said. "We've lathered, but now I think we need to rinse and repeat."

When the girls rinsed Wyatt a second time, he shook his head slightly. "Oh, no," Laila cried, recognizing what was about to happen. "Don't you do it!"

But Wyatt's small head shake quickly turned into a big head shake that traveled down his body and out the tip of his tail. The water from his coat showered the giggling girls who shielded their faces with their hands.

"Wyatt!" Ella scolded good-naturedly. "You send water flying like a four-legged hurricane! Next time I bathe you, I'll wear a raincoat!" Laila quickly draped him in the towel and rubbed vigorously. When she finished, the fur around his ears stood out in poofs.

"You're having a bad hair day, Wyatt," Ella said, reaching for a dog brush.

The girls continued to dry and brush until the puppy looked perfect. "You are adorable!" Ella said proudly. "But wait, something's missing."

Ella rummaged in the canvas bag she'd brought. "I was hoping I'd get a chance to use this." She pulled out a baby blue bow she'd bought for Coconut and fastened it around Wyatt's neck.

The girls beamed. "You look so handsome that people will fight for the chance to adopt you now!" Ella told him.

Wyatt cocked his head from side to side as though trying to understand what they were saying. Then he sat and gave his ear a good, long scratch. When he finished, his bubble-gum-pink tongue fell out of his mouth in a contented pant.

"He looks much happier now," Ella said.

"Yeah," Laila agreed. "He's smiling!"

The girls led Wyatt back to his kennel between the rows of barking dogs. But suddenly, the barking stopped, and the dogs stood still. A **bloodcurdling** scream echoed through the block building!

wyatt

10

OSCAR THE RAT

Wyatt scrambled behind Ella and Laila with his tail tucked between his legs. The scream rang out again and the girls whirled toward the source of the piercing sound. Ella couldn't believe her eyes when she saw Avery screaming and flailing her arms and legs like a scarecrow in a windstorm.

"Avery!" Ella yelled. "What's wrong?"

Avery screamed back, "Get it off! Get it off! Please get it off!"

"Get what off?" Ella asked in a panicked voice, wanting to help her sister but not understanding the problem.

Aniyah ran toward Avery with a small net. "I'll get him!" she yelled.

By this point, Eric and the Girl Scout leaders had heard the racket and ran to the rescue. Eric quickly realized what had happened when a small furry head popped out of the top of Avery's shirt.

"Oscar!" Eric scolded, pulling out a brown and white rat. The rat's whiskers twitched nervously, and Avery, pale as a ghost, looked like she might faint. She wrapped her arms tightly around her chest and shivered.

"Are you OK?" Aniyah asked. "I am sooooo sorry!"

"What happened?" Ella asked.

"We were cleaning his cage," Aniyah said. "It's divided in half. I shooed him into one side of his cage, but I didn't know the door was open on that side! He jumped out and headed straight for Avery's pants leg!"

"That...is...THE WORST...thing...that has EVER happened...to me!" Avery said and shivered again.

"I didn't know this shelter had rats!" Ella said.

"Only one," Eric answered while stroking the rodent's head with his thumb. "Someone left Oscar by our front door about a year ago. He loves people and sometimes he forgets his boundaries."

"I'm so sorry I let him escape," Aniyah cried. "If he'd gotten in with the cats, it would have been a disaster! I came to help the animals—not get them killed!"

Eric chuckled. "Don't worry," he said. "It's not your fault. I suspect he knows how to pick that lock on his cage. And as for the cats, he enjoys torturing them by running back and forth in front of their cages."

"Does he also enjoy torturing Girl Scouts?" Avery asked, her voice still trembling.

"Nope," Eric said. "You're the first!"

"Lucky me," Avery said, staring at the rat with disgust.

"You girls have done a great job today, and I hope you'll come back tomorrow," Eric said. "With the possibility of a storm coming, I'd like to get all the dogs walked. If the weather gets bad, they might have to stay inside for several days."

"Do you have enough food for the animals if the storm strikes?" Ella asked. She was hoping to find out more about the receipt she'd seen in the office.

"Yes, we have generous donors who keep us supplied with food," Eric said. "We never have to buy it."

He noticed Wyatt lying patiently by Ella's feet. "Wyatt!" he exclaimed. "You look like a show dog!" Wyatt's tail thumped the floor and he replied with a soft "Whoof!"

"He knows how good he looks," Laila said with a grin.

Later, when Mimi picked up the girls from the animal shelter, the girls were excited to tell her about their day's adventures. But Mimi's brows were pinched together in concern. She put her finger to her lips and turned up the radio. "Kevin has been upgraded to a Category 2 hurricane," the meteorologist announced. "Unless it turns, we can expect landfall in a day or so."

"Wow!" Avery said. "That's soon."

"Yes," Mimi agreed. "It's time to prepare."

Even though Ella could tell that Mimi was concerned, she was more interested in the mystery swirling in her mind than she was about the storm swirling out in the ocean. She motioned for a huddle in the back seat while Mimi listened to the weather forecast. She told Avery and Aniyah about finding the Crunchy Bones dog food receipt.

"That sounds like a coincidence," Avery said. "I doubt it has anything to do with our mystery."

"That's what I told her," Laila said.

"You heard him say that all the dog food is donated to the shelter, so why would he buy it?' Ella asked.

"Maybe he has a dog of his own," Aniyah suggested.

"Maybe," Ella replied. "But you'd think he would have mentioned his dog if he had one.

And did you see how uncomfortable he looked when he was asked about the missing dogs and Twila Simmons?"

"So, there's a missing kiddie pool, two dog food receipts—one with a note about Friday at 7:30—a red-headed boy next door with a dog, and the list of dog supplies dropped by an old lady in the fabric store," Avery said. "It's all so random, I'm not convinced any of those things are even clues."

"You're right," Ella said. "But what if they are? Dogs and puppies have mysteriously disappeared. They could be in a lot of danger! With the storm coming, we're running out of time! And what if more dogs disappear? I don't know what I'd do if Wyatt disappeared. He's the sweetest, cutest puppy ever!"

"Try not to worry," Laila said. "We're coming back to the shelter tomorrow and maybe we can find some more clues."

"I hope so," Ella said. "Forget what I said about something being fishy. Now, I smell a rat at that animal shelter, and his name's not Oscar!"

11

SNIFFS AND SCENTS

Ella awoke to the smell of sizzling bacon. She sat up in bed and rubbed her eyes. *Why is Mimi cooking bacon in the middle of the night?* She looked over at Avery's bed, which was neatly made. Hopping out of bed, she followed the scent to what looked like a red polar bear standing at the stove. It was flipping pancakes with one hand and turning bacon with the other.

Ella rubbed her eyes again. *Am I dreaming?* she wondered. The bear turned around and Ella realized it was Mimi in a fluffy robe and fuzzy slippers in her favorite color—red.

"It's about time you got up," Avery said from the kitchen table. "We've got to be back to the shelter in an hour."

"What?!" Ella asked. "Isn't it still night?"

Avery laughed. "It's just overcast," she said.

"Get used to it," Mimi said. "We'll have several days like this before the hurricane passes through."

"Is it safe to walk the dogs today?" Ella asked.

"Perfectly safe," Mimi answered. "We won't get any rain until tonight. Today is my prep day, though. After I drop you girls off at the shelter, I'm going shopping for all the supplies we'll need to weather the storm."

"What kind of supplies?" Ella asked.

"Flashlight batteries, bottled water, bread, milk, and some canned ravioli," Mimi said.

"That's a weird combo," Ella said.

"Well, we need to be able to see in the dark and have something to eat and drink if the electricity goes out," Mimi explained.

Coconut danced around Mimi's feet like a ballerina. "You are such a **vagabond** beggar,"

Mimi said. "But that reminds me I also need to pick up dog food and dog treats."

"Have you ever bought Crunchy Bones dog food?" Ella asked.

"Oh no," Mimi said. "Coconut only eats Princess Pets food."

About the time Mimi flipped a pancake, Coconut jumped and hit her leg, knocking her off balance. A fluffy pancake spun in the air and landed on Coconut's head like a flying saucer.

Coconut sniffed the air, confused about where the marvelous scent was coming from. She looked left and right.

Ella, Avery, Sadie, and Mimi laughed so hard that tears came to their eyes. "She looks like she's wearing a French beret!" Avery said between giggles.

"Oui, oui, Madame!" Ella said. "Would you like some butter and syrup on your beret?"

"Poor Coconut," Mimi said, flipping the pancake off her head, and breaking off a piece to give her a little nibble. "You're always good for a laugh!"

After breakfast, the girls slipped on their Girl Scout t-shirts and jeans. "Mrs. Brown said that any time we're doing something as a troop, people should know that we're Girl Scouts," Avery said.

When they arrived at the shelter, Eric met them with a somber face. "I'm afraid I've got bad news," he said. "When I got to work this morning, several more dogs were missing—Wyatt and his littermates."

"Did someone adopt them?" Ella asked.

"I wish," Eric said. "When I got here the building was locked, their kennels were open, and the puppies were gone, just like last time. It's like they disappeared into thin air." His voice trembled in distress.

"Just like the pool," Ella mumbled.

Laila and Aniyah walked in just in time to hear the bad news. "Maybe we didn't close the door correctly when we put Wyatt in," Laila said.

"Or maybe Oscar picked the locks and let them all out," Aniyah suggested.

"Oscar was snoozing in his locked cage this morning," Eric said. "He was exhausted from his big adventure yesterday. And even if Wyatt's cage wasn't closed correctly, he and the other puppies couldn't have gotten out of the building."

Tears welled in Ella's eyes. "I didn't solve the mystery, and now Wyatt is in trouble," she muttered.

"I've called the sheriff's office," Eric continued, "so we'll let them handle it. Let's concentrate on the dogs we still have. They could use a walk."

After the girls put on reflective Volunteer Dog Walker vests, Eric assigned each of them a dog.

"Remember the Girl Scout 'two by two' rule and stay with a buddy," Mrs. Brown cautioned. "And stay on the trail that makes a loop behind the animal shelter." She gave each girl a whistle and said, "Blow this whistle if you need an adult."

Ella was assigned a cream-colored puppy named Moppy that resembled a mop with legs. Laila's dog was Queenie, a tan hound dog that seemed more interested in sniffing the ground than walking. Avery's energetic terrier and Aniyah's mixed Doberman Pinscher puppy quickly led them far ahead of the younger girls.

"Let's go," Ella said to Laila as Moppy tugged at his leash. "What are we waiting for?"

"It's not me," Laila replied. She pointed at Queenie, whose nose was buried in a patch of goldenrods beside the trail.

"I've read that for dogs, discovering smells in their environment is like a trip to Disney World for us," Ella said.

"Come, on, Queenie!" Laila said, pulling the leash. "There's a lot more to smell ahead of us!"

"Maybe she can sniff out some clues to help us find the puppies," Ella said. "But I've got a hunch that Eric is involved. If the building was locked before and after the dogs disappeared, it has to be someone with a key."

As the girls continued along the trail, low, ghostly clouds whirled above them. Occasional rays of sun broke through and exploded into brilliant shimmers on the marshland in the distance. Gentle wind gusts made the Spanish moss beards hanging from trees look like old men gabbing about the approaching storm. The dogs seemed **ecstatic** to feel the wind in their faces and the dirt under their feet instead of concrete.

Queenie, finally moving at a decent pace, stopped to sniff around a bush, jerking Laila backwards. Moppy picked up the scent too, and the dogs led Laila and Ella in a dizzying parade around the bush. During one orbit, Ella brushed against the bush and something hit the ground. She reached down to pick it up.

"Laila!" she hollered. "Look at this!"

12

A BLUE CLUE

Ella held up a bright blue bow for Laila to see.

"That was Wyatt's bow!'" Laila exclaimed.

"It is!" Ella said, frowning. "We've got to find him!"

After circling the bush several more times, Queenie pulled Laila back to the trail. "I think she's following Wyatt's scent," Laila observed.

"Lead the way, Queenie!" Ella shouted.

Queenie, nose to the ground, followed the scent relentlessly. She trotted faster and faster until the girls and Moppy were running to stay with her. Finally, the old hound dog stopped where another path veered off the main trail. She whined as she looked at the girls and then looked down the path.

"She's lost the scent!" Laila said. "Why would it stop here?"

"Maybe Wyatt wasn't walking anymore," Ella said with a worried look on her face.

"You think they put him in a truck?" Laila asked.

"That path's too narrow for a truck," Ella answered.

"Alien spaceship?" Laila quipped.

"Laila, this is serious," Ella responded.

The girls pondered the situation while the dogs panted beside them. Ella looked through the trees to the marshland beyond and saw a strangely familiar house. *That's the creepy house I saw on the way to the animal shelter,* she thought.

Before she could point it out to Laila, Avery shouted to them from farther down the trail. "Ella! Come here quick!" Her voice echoed among the trees.

With the dogs leading the way, the girls raced to find Avery and Aniyah in a clearing. They looked puzzled.

"What is it?" Ella asked. "Did you find a clue?"

"Look," Avery said, motioning at the ground around her. She stood in an almost perfect circle of missing grass.

"Notice anything strange about this?" Avery asked.

Ella thought for a moment. She remembered what Mimi had said about the kiddie pool making circles on her lawn. "It's about the same size as our missing pool!"

"Exactly!" Avery answered. "But, look! There's more than one!"

Ella peered across the clearing to see at least ten circles cut out of the ground. Her mouth dropped open in amazement.

13

TIME TO HUNKER

As raindrops began to pelt the ground, Mrs. Brown called the girls back to the shelter with a bullhorn.

"What could have made those weird circles?" Ella asked as they scurried to the shelter.

"Spaceships," Laila said again. "They always make circles on the ground when they land."

"Now why would aliens come to Earth just to kidnap dogs?" Ella asked.

"Because their little green boys and girls need pets?" Laila suggested with a sly smile.

"I'm not much of a believer in aliens, but I don't have any better explanations at this point," Avery said. Her mind raced to make sense of it all.

Back at the shelter, Mrs. Brown explained that the hurricane would soon bear down on the coast. "It's time to get home and hunker down," she said.

"I don't know how to hunker," Ella said.

Mrs. Brown laughed. "That means to take shelter."

"Wouldn't the shelter be a safe place to stay?" Ella asked Eric. "We could make sure no one else kidnaps any animals."

Eric looked at his feet nervously. "It is a safe place for the animals," Eric said. "It was built on a hill that's high enough to be safe from the storm surge."

"What's storm surge?" Aniyah asked.

"Normally the tides go in and out..." Eric began.

"Everyone who lives near the coast knows that," Aniyah interrupted. "Tides are caused by the gravitational pull of the sun and moon."

"Right," Eric continued. "But when there's a hurricane, the tide comes in and the winds of the hurricane push even more water on top of the tide. The water has nowhere to go but inland and that causes storm surge flooding. It can be the most dangerous part of a hurricane."

Ella became even more concerned for her missing furry friends. *What if they were caught in the storm surge?* She thought of Wyatt's short puppy legs. *Did he even know how to dog paddle?*

Ella asked Eric, "What about all the animals?"

Eric folded his arms as he thought about his answer. "Well, if they're lucky," he said, "wild animals make it to higher ground or climb trees until the water recedes," he answered. "Unfortunately, a lot of pets are separated from their owners during hurricanes and wind up as strays. Sadly, many lose their lives."

The girls were quiet after hearing that sad news. Eric changed the subject. "Thanks again for all your help, everyone," he said. "I hope you'll volunteer again after the storm. I know that Juliette Gordon Low would be proud of the work you've been doing. You've all earned your pet badges, but I know that you haven't done it just for the badges. You've done it because you care about the animals."

Ella gave Moppy a big hug, led him into his kennel, and removed his leash. "Stay safe," she whispered. She pulled the metal door closed and made sure it locked. Moppy lay down with his head on his paws. He gave Ella such a sad look that she began to cry. "I promise I'll be back soon," she said softly.

"I'll put the leashes up," Ella told the other girls when they'd all put their dogs back in their kennels. Many of the dogs were barking. "If only dogs could talk," she added, draping the leashes over her shoulder. "Then they could tell us exactly what happened to the missing pups."

Ella went into the office to hang the leashes on the rows of hooks lining the back wall. The office window was splattered with rain, but a sudden movement caught her attention. She walked to the window and looked out. Through the distorted, watery view, she could see a boy carrying something in his hands. It looked like a long stick. The only thing she could tell for sure was that the boy had bright red hair.

14

CHOCOLATE BROCCOLI

When she picked them up at the shelter, Mimi informed the girls that Laila's grandmother had asked if Laila could stay with them. "She has an urgent errand to run before the storm hits," Mimi told Laila. "And your mother has to stay at the hospital until the storm passes through."

"Oh no," Ella said. "I didn't know your mother was in the hospital."

"She's a nurse," Laila explained. "She told me this morning that she'd probably have to stay at the hospital during the storm in case people get hurt and need help."

Ella's mind went to the missing puppies. "And animals," she murmured.

"Since Laila is staying with us, I called Aniyah's mother and got permission for her to stay as well," Mimi continued and looked at Aniyah. "That is, if she wants to."

"Are you kidding?" Aniyah said, grinning. "I'd love to!"

"Then it's official," Mimi said gleefully. "We are having a Girl Scout Hurricane Indoor Camporee! I even bought supplies to make indoor s'mores!"

The girls couldn't believe their eyes when they walked through Mimi's front door. In the family room, a pink tent and a blue tent were arranged around a make-believe campfire. The campfire was made with wads of brown paper "rocks" and red and yellow tissue paper "flames."

"Mimi!" Avery cried. "This is awesome!"

"We love it!" the others agreed and gave Mimi a group bear hug.

"This is my kind of camping," Aniyah exclaimed. "No bugs, no rain, and a short walk to the bathroom!"

Awakened by the excited voices, Coconut poked her head out of one of tents. She stretched out her front paws on the floor and opened her mouth in a huge yawn.

"Sorry we bothered you, Coconut!" Sadie said and laughed.

"Avery, why don't you and Ella grab some sleeping bags out of the garage so you girls can get settled before the hurricane hits and we lose power," Mimi said.

"Lose power?" Aniyah asked.

"There's a good possibility," Mimi said. "But don't worry. I have flashlights for each of you."

When Avery and Ella returned with the sleeping bags, Mimi was placing two fondue pots near the paper campfire. Sadie panicked when she lit the fire gel cans under the pots. "Mimi, don't!" she yelled.

"I have to light the fuel to melt the cheese and the chocolate or we can't have fondue," Mimi explained.

"But you'll catch our campfire on fire!" Sadie exclaimed.

Mimi laughed. "I promise I'll be careful!"

Once the contents of the fondue pots were melted, each of the girls chose a long fondue fork. Mimi brought in a tray of fruits and veggies, as well as marshmallows, pretzels, and crackers. "Coconut and I are going to my room to watch the weather reports," she told the girls. "Enjoy!"

"Good idea," Ella told Mimi. "If Coconut stays out here, she'll be dipping her tongue in the fondue for sure!"

"Yes, and dogs can't eat chocolate!" Laila remarked.

"Why not?" Aniyah asked.

"There's a substance in chocolate that dogs can't process the way humans can," Laila replied. "It can make them very sick if they eat too much. It can even kill them."

"Wow!" Aniyah exclaimed. "I can't imagine life without chocolate!"

The girls settled around their makeshift campfire. "This is almost as good as roasting marshmallows over a real campfire," Avery said, dipping a cube of bread into the gooey pot of cheese.

"Yeah," Ella agreed as she dunked a marshmallow into the cheese.

"The marshmallows go into the *chocolate*, Ella," Avery said, making a gagging sound. "Everyone knows that Girl Scouts love s'mores and that they're made with graham crackers, marshmallows, and chocolate. It's a classic combination."

"Well, this is a new flavor combo," Ella explained while smooshing the cheese-covered marshmallow between two saltine crackers. "This creation could earn me the Brownie Snacks badge at our next meeting. I'll call them ch'ores!" She opened her mouth wide to cram the concoction inside. "Hmmm, interesting...a little sweet, a little salty, a little savory. I'm on to something!"

"You've inspired me, Ella!" Aniyah said. "I hate broccoli, but if it was dipped in chocolate..."

"Please, no!" Avery yelled.

Aniyah plunged the broccoli spear into the molten chocolate, let it cool a moment, and crunched down. "Blaaaaah!" she exclaimed, swiftly grabbing a napkin and her glass of water.

"Are you OK?" Avery asked.

Aniyah guzzled all her water and said, "People say anything is good dipped in chocolate. Not true!"

The girls giggled and agreed that nothing green belonged in the melted chocolate pot.

After emptying both fondue pots, the girls lay on their sleeping bags with their heads poking out of their tents. "We should tell ghost stories," Aniyah suggested, propping her head in her hands.

"Ghost stories?" Sadie asked with wide eyes. "OK, I'm outta here," she said and scurried to Mimi's room.

"Who has time for ghost stories?" Ella said. "We still have a mystery to solve."

"I've been thinking," Laila said. "If those circles of missing grass were the same size as the pool, what could they be used for?"

"I'm not sure," Ella said. "But I've got a good idea who made those circles."

"You do?" Laila asked.

"The red-headed boy next door," Ella said. "I didn't tell you yet, but I saw him outside the animal shelter when I was hanging up the leashes. He had something in his hand. Maybe it was a shovel."

"Wait a minute," Avery said. "Isn't this Friday?"

"Yes, why?" Aniyah said.

"The receipt we found in the backyard—didn't it say Friday at 7:30?" Avery replied.

"Oh yeah, it did!" Ella said.

"What could anyone do tonight?" Laila asked. "There's a hurricane."

"I'm not sure," Ella said. "Maybe the red-headed boy is helping Eric take the dogs and puppies out of the animal shelter."

"Why would he steal dogs from his own shelter?" Aniyah asked.

"He told us he wants to be a veterinarian," Avery said. "That takes a lot of money. I've read there are people who take animals out of shelters and take them to other states to sell to people looking for pets. They can make a lot of money doing that."

"That might explain the dog food receipt in the shelter office," Ella said. "He'd have to take food to feed the dogs while he was taking them somewhere."

"I don't know," Avery said, exasperated. "We may be barking up the wrong tree. Eric seems like such a nice guy."

"Let's give it a rest," Aniyah suggested. "Thinking about it gives me a headache."

"I've got an idea," Ella said. "We could research Twila Simmons. I'd like to know more about her." Ella ran to Mimi's room and borrowed her laptop. The girls read several articles about the woman who loved animals enough to start the city's first shelter.

"It says here the shelter's board of directors asked her to resign when they felt she was too old to work at the shelter," Avery said. "They were afraid she would get hurt and sue the city for lots of money."

Avery found another article. "Look, here's an old picture of when they broke ground for the shelter."

Ella peered at the picture and then enlarged it. In the background of the picture, she could see the creepy old house she'd seen near the marsh. The difference was that it wasn't old and creepy when the photo was taken. She read the caption under the picture.

"It says Twila Simmons donated part of her family's land to build the shelter on," Ella said. "That must be her house!"

Suddenly, the lights flickered and the sound of rain on the roof stopped abruptly.

SCRATCH! SCRATCH! And something (or someone) was scratching at the window!

15

BONY FINGERS

The girls clicked on their flashlights and instinctively shined them toward the scratching sound. All they could see were the reflections of the lights on the window. "We've got to get closer to see outside," Avery said.

"OK-K-K," Aniyah stuttered. "You do that."

"What if it's the ghost of Mrs. Simmons?" Laila suggested.

"I thought we weren't telling ghost stories," Ella said. "Besides, why would an old lady be out in a hurricane? I'll look out the window."

Ella marched bravely to the window with the others close on her heels. She pressed her flashlight to the glass with one hand and cupped the other hand over her eyes to peer through the window.

"Is it h-h-her?" Laila asked through chattering teeth.

"I can't see anything," Ella said. "The window has too much rain on it."

A sudden gust of wind blew and tree limbs scraped against the windowpane like long, bony fingers. Startled, Ella jumped back, and all the girls screamed."

Mimi scampered out from her bedroom, where Sadie had already fallen asleep. "Are you girls OK?" she asked. The girls, huddled together, stared back at her.

"Don't be afraid, girls," Mimi said reassuringly. "It's just the wind. We can expect very strong winds soon. So, stay in the center of the room. That's the safest place to be during a hurricane in case flying debris knocks out a window. I'm going back to my room to monitor the weather radio. But don't worry. This house has withstood storms much stronger than this one."

The girls returned to their tents with the tree limbs clawing persistently at the window and sides of the house. They propped their flashlights together in the "campfire" so that the lights shined through the tissue paper flames. "It looks almost real," Aniyah observed.

The wind continued to gain speed until the house trembled in Hurricane Kevin's invisible grip. "It's just like those people being interviewed on the news always say," Ella remarked. "The hurricane does sound like a train." She held her knees and rocked back and forth as if the wind were blowing her too.

"I hope my grandmother's safe," Laila said. "I don't understand why she had an important errand to make during a hurricane!"

"I'm sure she's OK," Avery told her. "If she's anything like Mimi, she has a mind of her own, but she knows how to take care of herself."

"That wind is making me nervous," Aniyah admitted.

"Let's talk about something to keep our minds off it," Avery suggested.

"I know," Laila said. "Tell me about the badge ceremony. I'm the only person in the troop without a badge on her sash. I don't even have my Brownie pin yet!"

"Since we finished our volunteer project at the shelter, Mrs. Brown said we will have a Court of Awards ceremony," Avery explained. "Maybe she'll include an investiture ceremony as a part of it. That's when you'll get your pin. And I'm sure you'll earn a sash full of badges before you know it!"

"Thank you for saying that," Laila told the other girls. "I'm already starting to understand what it means to be a Girl Scout. I still miss Tucker, my sweet dog, but I at least I have sisters now."

After a group hug, Ella taught Laila the Brownie smile song. Avery and Aniyah, who remembered the song from their Brownie days, joined in. The girls sang loud enough to drown out the sounds of the storm raging outside.

The girls continued to sing and chat to keep their minds off the storm and off the missing puppies. Finally, everyone fell asleep but Ella. She tossed and turned in her tent, dreaming of puppy snatchers with long, bony fingers.

16

TURN AROUND, DON'T DROWN

"AAIIIEEEE!" Ella awoke to the scream coming from her own throat. A hand had grabbed her shoulder. Still unsure if she was awake or dreaming, she reached for her shoulder and touched Mimi's hand.

"I am sorry to startle you," Mimi said, "but you girls need to wake up."

"Is everything all right?" Avery asked, poking her head out of the tent and looking up to make sure the roof was still on the house. "Do we have to evacuate?"

"Nope. Everything's fine and dandy...at least it is here," Mimi replied. "The storm has passed through and aside from some broken tree limbs, we had no major damage. We may be without power for a day or two though."

"Then what's wrong?" Laila asked. "Are my mother and grandmother OK?"

"They are fine," Mimi replied. "Your mom has to remain at the hospital for now, and your grandmother had to stay in a hotel last night."

"I still don't understand what kind of errand took her out into a storm," Laila said.

"It was something very important," Mimi answered. "Please don't worry. I'm waking you girls because there are neighborhoods near the marshland that are now flooded."

"Because of the storm surge?" Ella asked.

"Exactly," Mimi answered. "Anyway, Mrs. Brown just called and said the animal shelter is open to take in animals displaced by the flooding. She asked if you girls would like to help."

"Yes! Yes!" Ella exclaimed.

"After all, 'Be prepared' is our motto," Avery remarked.

Aniyah nodded. "And that means that as Girls Scouts we are ready to help wherever needed—even in an emergency!"

"What does she need us to do?" Laila asked.

"I'm not sure," Mimi said. "But she will be by to pick you up soon."

The girls quickly dressed, rolled up their sleeping bags, and took down their tents. "Don't forget to douse the fire!" Ella said. She giggled as she removed the flashlights that had kept the "fire" aglow.

"My first Girl Scout campout was awesome," Laila exclaimed. "I can't wait to have more—maybe even one outside!"

"Friendship circle!" Avery commanded. Ella, Aniyah, and Avery quickly crossed their right arms over their left arms and joined hands. Laila looked confused. "What is a friendship circle?" she asked.

"It's what Girl Scouts usually do at the end of a meeting," Ella explained as she grabbed Laila's hand. "It represents the unbroken chain of friendship among all Girl Scouts."

"Yes," Ella added. "Now we each make a silent wish and pass it by squeezing the hand you're holding so that it goes around the circle. I have a feeling that each of our wishes will have something to do with saving puppies."

"That's really sweet, girls," Mimi remarked. "And since you were talking about circles, I've got some tasty circles for breakfast."

"Donuts!" the girls shouted.

"You are correct!" Mimi said, opening a bakery box filled with assorted donuts. "It certainly can't be pancakes since I have no electricity to cook them."

"You're just like a Girl Scout," Ella told Mimi as she chose a donut with pink frosting and sprinkles, "always prepared!"

Soon, the girls heard a loud horn in the driveway. Mimi peeked out and announced, "It's Mrs. Brown. Time to go rescue some puppies. Be careful!"

"Is Sadie coming?" Ella asked Mimi.

"No," Mimi answered. "I'm letting her sleep in and keep me company today."

The girls scrambled out the door and sloshed across the saturated ground to pile into Mrs. Brown's SUV. Two other Girl Scouts were already buckled in the back seat. As they backed out of the driveway, something caught Ella's eye. The red-haired boy next door was hooking a small trailer to an all-terrain vehicle. A bright yellow kayak sat on the trailer.

"I guess he's taking advantage of the flood waters to go kayaking," Ella whispered to Avery sarcastically.

Before Avery could comment, Mrs. Brown began explaining their mission for the day. "Eric called me from the shelter this morning, girls," she explained. "He said that a lot of dogs are coming in because of the storm and flood waters. He needs all the help he can get."

Ella was puzzled. "How are the dogs being rescued?" Ella asked. "And how do they get to the shelter?"

Mrs. Brown knew the answer to both questions. "Emergency personnel and volunteers are out rescuing people who are stranded. Those same people are also rescuing any animals they find. Plus, good Samaritans are bringing lost pets to the shelter, hoping their owners will come and claim them."

"I hope someone can find all the animals that disappeared from the shelter *before* the storm," Ella said.

"So do I," Mrs. Brown said. "But it's funny— If they hadn't disappeared, there wouldn't be room at the shelter for the animals who need it now."

"Hmmm, I never thought about that," Ella said.

On their way to the shelter, Mrs. Brown took an alternate route to avoid areas of flooding and roads blocked by fallen trees. Although the hurricane had proceeded on its track northward, the early morning sky was streaked with retreating clouds that looked like great, rocky cliffs. The feeble sunlight cast an eerie orange glow, while occasional wind gusts made tired trees dance like tortured spirits. Tree limbs, roof shingles, and other debris littered the area like waste from a spilled trash can.

"The roadsides look like little rivers!" Laila exclaimed as she and Ella watched the water racing beside the road.

"That's why it's important to be very careful about where we drive," Mrs. Brown said. "Always remember the rule: Turn around, don't drown."

"What does that mean?" Aniyah asked.

"If you try to drive through water," Mrs. Brown explained, "it's hard to tell how deep it is. Your vehicle could be swept away. It only takes about 12 inches of water to wash away a car. Water is a very powerful force."

Suddenly Ella yelled, "STOP!"

17

PUPPY RESCUE

Mrs. Brown slammed on the brakes. "Ella, what in the world is it?"

"There," Ella yelled. "In the ditch! That dog is in trouble!"

"Oh my goodness!" Mrs. Brown shouted when she spotted a dog's head bobbing in the storm water. "He must be caught in the storm drain."

"We have to help him," Laila cried.

"Stay calm, girls," Mrs. Brown cautioned. "Frightened animals are dangerous."

"Shouldn't we call the police or the fire department?" one of the other Girl Scouts suggested.

"All the emergency personnel are overwhelmed right now," Mrs. Brown explained. "We'll have to handle this ourselves. Avery and Aniyah, there's a rope in the back. Would you get it, please?"

Mrs. Brown opened the door and climbed out of the SUV. "Stay behind me," she told the girls as she motioned to them to follow.

When Avery handed her the rope, Mrs. Brown tied it around her waist. She quickly tied the other end to the trailer hitch. The trapped dog yapped in terror and desperation.

"Please hurry!" Ella urged.

"You girls can hang on to the rope, but just make sure it stays attached to the trailer hitch," Mrs. Brown said. She inched her way into the muddy water that swirled around her ankles and stretched her arms toward the dog. He looked at her with wild eyes and yelped even louder.

"I can't reach him," she said, wading further into the ditch.

The girls gripped the rope with all their strength, trying to help Mrs. Brown. They feared she could fall and be swept away by the water.

"It's OK, honey," Mrs. Brown cooed, just loud enough for the dog to hear her above the sound of rushing water. "We're here to help you. Don't be scared."

The dog stopped yelping and struggled toward her, clawing at the water with his front paws. With the water swirling higher around her legs, Mrs. Brown eased around to his side. Cautiously, she stroked the terrified dog's soaked head and ran her hand down his back. "His back leg is caught," she said, reaching under the water and into the drain pipe. When she had a firm grip, she ordered the girls, "Pull!"

The girls tugged as hard as they could on the rope, pulling Mrs. Brown as she pulled the dog. "Once more," she said. "Pull!"

After one last effort, Mrs. Brown exclaimed, "He's free!" She grabbed the dog in a bear hug. The girls kept pulling, putting all their weight into it until Mrs. Brown stumbled up onto the road.

"You did it!" the girls cheered. "You saved the dog!"

"No," Mrs. Brown corrected. "*We* did it— Girl Scout style! See what we can accomplish when we all work together?"

Avery ran back to the SUV and grabbed a blanket which Mrs. Brown wrapped around the trembling dog. "Awww, he's still a puppy," Mrs. Brown said. "Probably seven or eight months old. You are one lucky little brindle," she told him.

"What's a brindle?" Aniyah asked. "I've never heard of that breed of dog."

"It's not a breed," Mrs. Brown explained. "It's a color pattern of tan or red with black stripes, almost like a tiger except the stripes are not as distinct. Now, let's get this pup to the shelter. Maybe his owners will come looking for him there."

Cradling the cold, wet puppy as they rode to the shelter, Ella looked him over carefully. "I wonder if he was one of the pups that disappeared from the shelter," she remarked.

"I don't remember seeing one that looked like that," Avery said. "But it's hard to be sure."

When they arrived at the shelter, the girls couldn't believe their eyes. Not only were each of the kennels full, but portable crates were jammed into every available spot. They held frightened dogs and cats barking and meowing. Anxious owners had already arrived at the shelter looking for their lost pets.

Tears streamed down the cheeks of one little girl in a wheelchair. "Baxley's not here," she said to her parents between sobs.

Ella, who was carrying the rescued pup in her arms, noticed that he pricked up his ears at the sound of the little girl's voice. "Do you know her, boy?" Ella asked. The dog squirmed in her arms and when she placed him on the floor, he took off. Before Ella could catch him, he had leaped into the wheelchair and was furiously licking the little girl's face.

"Baxley!" the little girl cried. "You found me!" Her tears continued to flow, except now they were tears of joy.

Ella's own eyes welled with tears at the happy reunion. Her thoughts turned to Wyatt. She quickly surveyed the caged dogs of every color, size, and shape, hoping she could experience a happy reunion like the little girl. But Ella wasn't as lucky.

18

RUNAWAY RESCUE

Eric asked the Girl Scout volunteers to make sure that every new animal in the shelter had plenty of fresh water and food.

As the girls made their rounds, Ella told Laila, "Let's check on Queenie and Moppy."

The girls walked past the kennels now filled with rescued animals. But when they reached Moppy's kennel, it was occupied by a white bulldog. "He's gone," Ella said sadly.

"So is Queenie," Laila reported.

Soon, Avery and Aniyah joined them and reported that the dogs they walked the day before were gone as well.

"How could every single dog that was already in the shelter disappear, and then the shelter fills up with more dogs?" Ella asked. "I don't understand it!"

"Someone must have come last night at 7:30 p.m., like the note said," Avery suggested.

"You're right," Ella agreed. "That was before the storm got too bad."

When Ella went to get more dog food, she noticed empty pegs where leashes had hung the day before. She stepped inside the office for a closer look and saw a scrap of paper on the floor. It said:

kiddie pool

dog toys

leashes

Ella hurried back with the dog food and showed the list to Avery. "Look at this, Avery! Whoever took the dogs took our kiddie pool!"

"Really? That's so weird!" Avery exclaimed. "But why?"

The girls were interrupted by the sound of Aniyah fussing at a yappy Dachshund. She had opened the crate to slide in some food. Suddenly, he darted past her and headed straight for the shelter's back door, which someone had propped open.

"Catch him!" Aniyah yelled.

The girls chased the little wiener dog out the back door and watched him dash down the now muddy trail behind the shelter. They followed as fast as they could until their shoes were weighed down with sticky mud.

"I don't...see him...anymore!" Aniyah cried, breathless from running. "Maybe...we should go back...and get help!"

"No!" Ella said, wiping her feet on the wet grass beside the trail. "Then we'll never catch him."

The girls continued to plod along the muddy trail, following the dog's tiny tracks. When they reached the bush where they'd found Wyatt's blue bow, they saw that the little dog's tracks had turned down the narrow path beside it.

"There's something about this trail," Ella said. "This is where Queenie stopped, remember?"

"We shouldn't go down there," Avery said. "That might bring us too close to the salt marsh and the flooding. Remember, turn around, don't drown."

"We *will* turn around if we get to water," Ella said. "Let's follow it as far as we can."

"OK," Avery said. "But I'll lead. I've got my cell phone to call for help if we get into trouble."

The girls continued down the path until marsh grass flanked them on either side. Before long, water had spread to the sides of the path."

"This must be flood water," Avery said. "We should go back."

"But what about the Dachshund?" Aniyah asked.

"We'll send someone back in a boat to look for him," Avery answered.

Reluctantly, the girls turned back. But when they had backtracked a short distance, they were horrified to see that water had already covered the trail behind them.

"We're cut off!" Ella said. "We have to keep following the path."

Avery quickly pulled out her cell phone and called Mrs. Brown to explain their situation.

"She's sending help," Avery said.

"The water's rising quickly," Laila said shakily, watching it slowly creep around their shoes.

"We have to keep going forward," Ella said. "Maybe we can find higher ground."

The path continued to narrow until the girls were putting one foot in front of the other as if they were walking a tight rope to stay out of the water.

"Do you hear that?" Ella asked.

"Is it our rescue boat?" Aniyah asked hopefully.

"No," Ella answered. "It's barking dogs!"

The girls listened carefully. "It sounds like it's coming from up the path, just around that little island of scrubby trees," Avery observed.

As soon as the path rounded the patch of trees, the girls got a clear view of where the sound was coming from. "It's that house!" Ella cried. "The Twila Simmons house!"

"That place looks super creepy!" Aniyah said. "I don't want to go there."

"I've got a hunch," Ella said. "We've got to go. Besides, it's on higher ground."

The girls nervously made their way to the huge old house.

"Look at that kayak!" Ella said. "It looks like the one the red-haired boy next door to Mimi was hauling this morning."

The sound of barking dogs grew louder as the girls stepped onto the creaky porch steps.

"Can't we just wait here for our rescue boat?" Laila begged. "Please don't knock on that door."

But Ella was already knocking.

The door creaked open and an elderly lady peeked out. "What are you girls doing here?" she asked in a squeaky voice. "Don't you know it's not safe to be near a tidal creek after a hurricane? The water is rising."

"We lost a dog," Ella answered. "We thought maybe he came here, since we heard lots of dogs barking."

"It's impossible to keep them quiet," the old lady said. "You might as well take a look here for your missing dog."

Clinging tightly to each other, the girls stood at the open door and gasped.

19

PUPPIES, PUPPIES EVERYWHERE!

Ella could not believe her eyes. Lining the walls of the huge living room were kiddie pools filled with sod. Dogs wandered everywhere— grown dogs, sweet little puppies, dogs of every color and shape.

But what caught Ella's eye was a bundle of fluffy yellow Lab puppies in the corner. "Look at that!" she exclaimed hopefully. At the sound of her voice, one of the little heads popped up. "Wyatt!" Ella exclaimed as the yellow ball of fluff leaped over his littermates and barked at her joyfully. "You're safe!"

"These are the dogs that disappeared from the shelter!" Avery exclaimed.

"They are!" Laila agreed. "I see Moppy and Queenie."

"Ma'am, are you Twila Simmons?" Ella asked cautiously.

"Yes," the old lady answered.

"But why did you steal the dogs?" Laila asked.

Ella spoke before Ms. Simmons had a chance. "I think I know," Ella said. "You wanted to move them to a safe place so there would be plenty of room at the shelter for other dogs after the storm."

"My dear, you are exactly right," Ms. Simmons said. "When I was a little girl, I lost my beloved dog during a hurricane. I wanted to save others from that pain."

"And that's why you were at the fabric store getting blanket material," Ella said. "You wanted to make the dogs comfortable while they stayed with you. We found your list!"

"Oh yes," Ms. Simmons said. "There were lots of supplies to gather. Thankfully, I had lots of help from my grandson."

"Does he have red hair, by any chance?" Ella asked. She already knew the answer to her question.

"Yes, he does," Ms. Simmons said. She called up the stairs, "Brad, come down here, please!"

In a moment, the red-haired boy the girls had seen through the fence came down the stairs. He was holding a Dachshund wrapped up in a towel.

"Hey! That's the dog that ran from the shelter and led us here," Aniyah said.

"I was out in my kayak looking for animals in trouble," Brad said. "This little guy was in the water, struggling to stay afloat."

"Thanks for saving him!" Aniyah said.

Ella asked Ms. Simmons, "How did you get into the animal shelter?"

"After the board of directors asked me to resign, I kept my key," Ms. Simmons said. "I know it wasn't right, but the shelter was such a big part of my life for so long that I couldn't give it up. They said I was too old, but the dogs didn't seem to think so. Almost every night after everyone left, I'd sneak down there to visit the animals and take them treats."

"And you took our kiddie pool?" Avery asked.

"That was me," Brad admitted. "My grandmother sent me to the store to buy some, but it was so late in the season, they were hard to find. I "borrowed" yours, but I promise I was going to return it as soon as I could."

"And you dug all those circles of sod?" Avery asked.

"Yes," Brad said, "to go inside the pools."

"But what are they for?" Ella asked.

"Puppy porta potties," Ms. Simmons said. "All these puppies needed a place to potty while they were visiting me."

Ella's face crinkled. "That's a great idea, but...I don't think I want our pool back."

Despite the noisy puppies, the girls soon heard Mrs. Brown's voice coming from the bullhorn of a boat outside. They ran to the porch to assure her they were safe.

"The water here is rising quickly," Mrs. Brown told them. "We have to go."

"We have to help Ms. Simmons get all these puppies upstairs in case the water reaches the house," Ella told the girls.

After explaining the situation to Mrs. Brown, the Scouts worked quickly to help Brad and Ms. Simmons get the puppies and their supplies to the safety of the second floor."

"We'll send the authorities to check on you," Mrs. Brown promised as she and the girls pulled away.

"Thank goodness for the Girl Scouts!" Ms. Simmons said. "We couldn't have done it without you!"

20

A GOOD WIND

Two days after the puppy rescue, Ella and Avery awoke to the sound of the weather report blaring from Mimi's family room.

"It's going to be a beautiful, sunny autumn day, folks," the meteorologist exclaimed.

"Hurray!" Ella shouted, flipping on a light switch. "The power's back on!"

"And I smell pancakes!" Avery cried, jumping out of bed and running to the kitchen.

"Good morning, girls," Mimi said cheerfully. "Things are finally getting back to normal around here."

"Arf, arf!" Coconut barked at the girls and danced on her hind legs.

"Good morning, Coconut," Ella said. "It looks like a beautiful day for a bath!" She giggled at the thought. Coconut whimpered and ran under the couch to hide.

"Just kidding!" Ella said. "Your fur's almost white again anyway. I'm really sorry that your couch isn't, Mimi."

"It's OK," Mimi said. "I'm starting to like it that way—it's a work of art."

"Speaking of art, I have a surprise for you!" Avery said.

"Ooooh!" Mimi said, rubbing her hands together in anticipation. "I love surprises!"

"Since Coconut created a one-of-a-kind design on your couch, I thought you should have one-of-a-kind artwork to hang over it." Avery pulled a painting from behind the couch where she'd hidden it. "This is the painting that I thought Coconut had ruined," she began. "But I decided to turn lemons into lemonade. Or in this case, I guess it would be 'turn Coconut's escapade into lemonade.' Anyway, here it is!"

Avery turned the painting around to reveal a beautiful autumn tree, except the leaves weren't really leaves. She had dipped Coconut's paw into paint and used her paw prints as leaves on the tree.

"Oh, Avery, I love it!" Mimi cried as she squeezed her granddaughter in a bear hug. "You and Coconut are the best artists I know!"

Sadie clapped with delight. "I want to draw a picture for Mimi too!" she exclaimed.

"That is really pretty, Avery," Ella said, but her smile quickly faded.

"Are you OK?" Mimi asked.

"I am just worried about all the puppies at Ms. Simmons' house and the shelter," she said.

"I have great news about that," Mimi announced. "I read an article in today's paper that the board of directors have asked Ms. Simmons to return to the shelter as honorary director! And she has also donated money to build another wing onto the shelter. So now, there will always be a place for homeless dogs—even after a natural disaster."

"That's awesome!" Ella cried.

After breakfast, the girls dressed in their full Daisy, Brownie, and Girl Scout uniforms. Mrs. Brown had called a special meeting at the community center.

"I want you to know how very proud I am of you," Mrs. Brown remarked. "You worked hard to help animals in need. You made a difference! Each of you has earned your pet care badge. Now, I have a special friend who would like to present those badges."

From the back of the meeting room, Eric led Wyatt toward the girls. Wyatt trotted down the center aisle of the community center, wearing a sash around his fuzzy yellow body with all the badges attached to it. The girls laughed and applauded. Eric handed a badge to each of the girls, but saved Ella's badge for last. When he finally called her name, he gave her the badge and then handed her Wyatt's leash.

Ella was confused. "Do you want me to take him for a walk?" she asked.

"Yes, I do," Eric said. "Every day! Because he's yours now."

Ella stared at him in stunned silence, her mouth wide open. She looked at Mimi, who nodded approvingly. "He's yours," Mimi repeated. "You have your parents' permission!"

With tears streaming down her face, Ella hugged Wyatt tightly. "I'll take such good care of you!" she whispered to him. Wyatt licked her cheek as his tail wagged furiously from side to side.

Laila, who was just watching the ceremony since she was not officially a member, cheered loudly. "And finally," Mrs. Brown said, "we are going to have an Investiture Ceremony for a Brownie who hasn't received her pin. Laila, would you please come forward?"

Laila smiled broadly as she hurried up to the podium. After completing the ceremony to make Laila a Brownie, Mrs. Brown had another surprise.

"Now, Laila," Mrs. Brown announced, "there is someone special here to present your pin and the pet care badge that you've already earned."

Laila's grandmother stepped out from the back of the community center. She led a black and white dog with fuzzy ears and freckles on his nose. Like Wyatt, the dog wore a sash that held Laila's pin and badge. Laila burst into tears upon seeing the dog. "Tucker? Tucker? Is that really you?" she cried. The dog, half-barking and half-whimpering, raced to Laila, jumping up to lick her face.

"Oh, I get it now!" Avery exclaimed. "So that was the important errand Laila's grandmother had to do during the hurricane. She had found Tucker and was bringing him back to Laila!"

Ella led Wyatt up to meet Tucker, and hugged Laila. "As bad as Hurricane Kevin was, he blew in some good things too!" Ella whispered to her new best friend. "We both found our 'furever' friends!"

The End

Tucker

Ella and Sadie with their puppy

About the Author

 Carole Marsh is the Founder and CEO of Gallopade International, an award-winning, woman-owned family business founded in 1979 that publishes books and other materials intended to guide, inspire, and inform children of all ages. Marsh is best known for her children's mystery series called **Real Kids! Real Places! America's National Mystery Book Series.**

During her 30 years as a children's author, Marsh has been honored with several recognitions including Georgia Author of the Year and Communicator of the Year. She has also received the iParenting Award for Greatest Products, the Excellence in Education Award, and been honored for Best Family Books by *Learning* Magazine. She is also the author of *Mary America, First Girl President of the United States,* winner of the 2012 Teacher's Choice Award for the Family from *Learning* Magazine.

For more information about Carole Marsh and Gallopade International, please visit www. gallopade.com.

TALK ABOUT IT!

Book Club Discussion Questions
for a Class or Girl Scout Troop

1. At the beginning of the story, Ella tried to help Mimi by giving her dog a bath. Although her intentions were good, things didn't turn out well. Have you ever tried to do something kind that didn't turn out well? What did you do?

2. Who was your favorite character in the book? What did you like best about that character? What was the funniest part of the story? Did it make you laugh out loud?

3. At her first Girl Scout meeting, Laila felt very shy and uncomfortable since she didn't know anyone. Have you ever been in a situation like that? How did you feel? Have you ever helped a newcomer feel welcome?

4. If you had the choice between buying any kind of dog you want or adopting a dog from an animal shelter, which would you choose to do? Explain your choice.

5. Would you like to volunteer at an animal shelter like the girls in the story? If so, what would you most like to do to help?

6. In the story, the girls had to ride out a hurricane. Have you ever experienced a hurricane or powerful storm? Were you afraid? What did you do to pass the time during the storm?

7. A move forced Laila to leave something she loved behind—her dog. Have you ever had to give up something that you cared deeply about?

8. Did you learn anything about dogs while reading this story? What is the most interesting thing you learned? Would you like to do more research to learn more about dogs? Would you someday like to work with dogs? Would you prefer to be a veterinarian or a dog trainer?

9. Do you have a dog or other pet? Does your pet ever make you feel better when you're feeling sad? If your answer is yes, explain why that happens.

10. Avery thought her painting was ruined, but she turned it into something unique in the end. Has there ever been a time when you turned a mess into a masterpiece?

BRING IT TO LIFE!

Book Club Activities for a Class or
Girl Scout Troop

1. Coconut was a mixed-breed dog. Use colored pencils, crayons, or markers to draw a picture of a dog that is a mix of all your favorite dog breeds. Make sure to give your special dog an interesting name.

2. In the story, the girls had fun tasting different items dipped in cheese and chocolate at their indoor campout. With an adult's help, melt cheese and chocolate in a microwave oven or a fondue pot and have your own tasting party! Make a chart to record your favorites and the items you disliked.

3. Purchase fleece fabric like the girls in the story to make blankets to donate to an animal shelter near you. Cut the fabric into a 30X30-inch square (or make it larger

for larger animals.) Use scissors to make two-inch-wide slits around the fabric. Cut the four corners out. Next, cut each two-inch slit in half and tie it in a double knot.

4. The girls met Wyatt at the animal shelter. Write a story about Wyatt's life before he came to the animal shelter.

5. Use non-toxic paint such as tempera to paint a dog's paw. Use that paw as your inspiration to paint a one-of-a-kind tree or other design using dog paws.

6. Play charades with balloons. Place notes inside balloons with the names of different animals on them. Blow up the balloons. Stand in a circle and play some music while passing the balloon from person to person. Have someone stop the music. The person holding the balloon must pop it and imitate the animal on the note. The other players must guess what animal it is.

SCAVENGER HUNT

Let's go on a Scavenger Hunt! See if you can find the items below related to the mystery, and then write the page number where you found each one. *(Teachers and Girl Scout Leaders: You have permission to reproduce this page for your students/Girl Scouts.)*

_____ 1. dog shampoo

_____ 2. Spanish moss

_____ 3. a green balloon

_____ 4. corn dogs

_____ 5. a canvas bag

_____ 6. a rat

_____ 7. fuzzy slippers

_____ 8. a bright blue bow

_____ 9. fondue pots

_____ 10. a yellow kayak

SAT GLOSSARY

bloodcurdling: causing terror or horror

cantankerous: bad-tempered, argumentative, and uncooperative

ecstatic: feeling or expressing overwhelming happiness or joyful excitement

remnants: pieces of cloth or carpeting left when the greater part has been used or sold

vagabond: a person, usually without a permanent home, who wanders from place to place

Enjoy this exciting excerpt from:

THE COOKIE THIEF Girl Scout MYSTERY

by Carole Marsh

1

LOOKIE, LOOKIE, WE'VE GOT COOKIES!

"This makes me so mad! I can't get this cookie to fit over my head," Ella grumbled. She hopped around her bedroom, trying to force a cardboard cutout of a caramel cookie over her head and shoulders.

"I think you're supposed to *step* into it," Ella's friend Annie suggested. Her dark, silky brown hair was woven into a loose braid tied with a green ribbon. The ribbon glittered with multicolored sprinkled cookies printed all over it. The colors popped against her olive skin. Annie wore an empty shortbread cookie box over her waist held up with red suspenders.

"Well, you could have told me that before I got my shoulders stuck!" Ella complained. She yanked the cookie cutout off her head and stepped into the hole in the middle, easily pulling it up to her waist. "There! A cookie skirt!"

Ella and Annie twirled around to admire their outfits in Ella's full-length mirror. Along with the "cookie skirt," Ella wore polka-dotted socks pulled up to her knees, her Girl Scout vest, and the same cookie-print ribbon in her long, straight blond hair as Annie had. Annie wore cutouts of different types of Girl Scout Cookies pinned to her shirt. Both girls grabbed noisemakers made out of empty milk bottles filled with beans.

"I think we're ready!" Ella exclaimed. She was proud of their creative outfit ideas!

"Whoa! You two are really taking this parade thing seriously." Ella's older sister Avery burst into Ella's room without knocking, again. Her blonde hair flew into the air as she bounced onto Ella's bed.

Ella felt her cheeks turn red. "We're dressed for the cookie rally! I thought you and Kate were dressing up too!"

"Usually only the Brownies dress in silly outfits," Avery replied. She and her friend Kate eyed each other and laughed.

Ella considered wriggling out of her "cookie skirt." She didn't want to look like a silly, naive Brownie. She glanced back into the mirror and changed her mind. "I think we look cute," she declared.

"It's almost time!" Annie's excited announcement interrupted Ella's thoughts. "The rally starts in ten minutes." Annie grabbed Ella's hand with a squeal and pulled her out of the bedroom.

The girls headed downstairs to a living room full of other Girl Scouts. Ella and Avery had volunteered their house as the meeting place for their cookie parade. They lived two blocks from the community center where a giant cookie rally party was set up. Their troop planned to host a mini parade from Ella and Avery's house to the community center to mark the kick-off of cookie-selling season. Mimi and Papa, the girls' grandparents, had offered to chaperone the parade. They were visiting from their home in South Carolina. Mimi wrote children's mystery books for a living and always had a flair for the dramatic. She had spent all day decorating the community center with other volunteers. Ella couldn't wait to see what it looked like.

"OK, Girl Scouts, let's line up!" called Mrs. Graham, Ella and Avery's troop leader. She waved her hands over her head to direct the girls to the front door. "We will proceed youngest to oldest, so Brownies first."

Ella and Annie scrambled to the front of the line with the other Brownies, their noisemakers poised high in the air. The older scouts filed in behind them, including Avery and Kate. While she wasn't as excited as her little sister was, Avery couldn't hide the smile that spread across her face. Cookie-selling season was her favorite part about being a Girl Scout!

"Let's go!" Mrs. Graham opened the door and stepped out in an animated march. She led the girls along the sidewalk toward the community center. Several chaperones, including Mimi and Papa, walked on either side of the Girl Scouts to make sure they were safe.

Ella and Annie shook their noisemakers as hard as they could above their heads. One of the Junior Scouts yelled, "Lookie, lookie, we've got cookies!" The others echoed the cheer over and over as they marched down the sidewalk. Several drivers passing by honked their horns in support. Others leaned out their windows and waved to the girls.

Papa grinned and tipped his black cowboy hat in reply. "Just moving these little cowpokes along to their cookie party," he called to the drivers. Mimi laughed. "Remember, it's not about you, Papa," she said. "It's all about the cookies!"

Ella was breathless with excitement when the girls arrived at the community center.

"That was so much fun!" Annie squealed. "We should have parades more often!"

"And it's not over yet," Ella added. "We still get to go to the cookie rally. I can't wait to see what Mimi did with the decorations. Believe me, it'll be good!"

Annie and Ella grinned as Mrs. Graham pulled open the double doors of the community center. "Welcome to our 10th annual Girl Scout Cookie Rally!" she announced.

2

AUNTIE MANURE

Ella sucked in a deep breath as the doors opened. The community center had several small rooms situated around one massive gymnasium used for community sports, parties, and political events. But Ella had never seen the gym like this before. Colorful banners for each ranking of Girl Scouts draped the walls of the gym. Ella quickly found the brown Brownie banner and gathered under it with the other Brownies. Avery and Kate headed toward the green Junior banner. Twinkling multicolored lights hung from the ceiling, adding a warm feeling to the normally plain gym. A Girl Scout logo made of banner paper was taped to the wall in the middle of the other banners.

A long table in the center of the gym held a huge spread of food. Ella's eyes feasted on saucy meatballs, pigs in a blanket, crispy chicken nuggets, vegetable trays, a colorful fruit platter, and plates of every kind of Girl Scout Cookie.

"That's a lot of cookies!" Ella whispered to Annie.

Smaller tables dotted the outer walls of the gym. Each was decorated with a different cookie-related theme.

"Welcome Girl Scouts, families, and friends!" Mrs. Graham stood under the Girl Scout banners with a microphone. "We are so excited for a new season of cookie selling! This Cookie Rally is our way of kicking off this exciting season and letting the community know that the Girl Scout Cookies are FINALLY HERE!" Mrs. Graham said the last words in a high-pitched sing-song voice, and the crowd in the gym cheered.

"Please enjoy some great food," Mrs. Graham added. "We invite our Girl Scouts to visit all of our cookie-selling stations set up around the room. Each table has a special ribbon you can pin to your vest to show you completed your cookie-selling prep courses. Remember, you're never too old to review the best ways to sell our delicious Girl Scout Cookies!" Mrs. Graham looked at Avery and Kate's group with a smile.

"OK, now, go have fun!" Mrs. Graham excitedly applauded and the rest of the gym joined her.

"Where should we go first?" Annie asked. She grabbed Ella's hand and they scanned the room together.

"THERE!" Ella exclaimed. She pointed to a table in the corner decorated with a bright red tablecloth dotted with glitter and sparkly red balloons. "That has got to be the table Mimi decorated!"

As the girls neared the table, they spotted a sign above it that said, "Cookie Selling Safety Tips." Mimi stood behind the table in a red sequin top with a shiny gemstone cookie pinned just below her right shoulder.

"Mimi! Your table looks great," Ella said.

"Thank you, sweetie." Mimi leaned down and gave Ella a big kiss on the cheek, leaving behind a bright red lipstick mark. Ella quickly wiped her cheek with her sleeve.

"My table is all about cookie-selling safety," Mimi explained. "I picked this theme because it's so important to me that my little angels are safe!"

"Are these safety rules like you should look both ways before crossing the street?" asked Annie.

"Sure, that could be one," Mimi said, "but there are others too. There are some really important ones

156

like always wear your Girl Scout uniform when selling cookies so that people know who you are. Another rule is always have a buddy when selling cookies. You never do it alone."

Annie and Ella looped elbows and grinned up at Mimi.

"Good, I see you've already found a buddy," Mimi said. "Here's a handout that lists some of our most important rules." Mimi handed the girls a brochure with safety tips.

"It says here to partner with adults, too," Ella read.

"That's right! That's why I volunteered to chaperone," Mimi announced with a smile. "I get to go with you when you sell cookies door-to-door."

Ella wasn't sure if she was excited or disappointed. She loved being with Mimi, but she was looking forward to being a grown-up, independent Girl Scout.

"Don't worry, I'll let you do all the work," Mimi said. She winked at Ella. "Here, take the brochure with you and review the safety rules before you start selling. And here are your ribbons!" Mimi handed both girls a gold button with a sparkly red ribbon attached. The button read "SAFETY RULES." Annie and Ella proudly pinned the button to their vests and headed to the next table.

An hour later, Annie and Ella had ribbons all over their vests and a handful of handouts. They had visited tables featuring how to handle money, how to market their cookie selling, how to set cookie-selling goals, and how to use the digital cookie app.

Ella stared down at a handout that looked like a game board. Each step of the cookie-selling process was mapped out on the sheet, from goal setting to how to use your cookie money. The steps in between included holding a meeting with family and friends, finding good cookie-selling spots, and tracking your progress.

I hope I can do this, Ella thought.

"Man, this is a lot more work than I thought," Annie commented.

Ella nodded, "It's almost like running a business!"

"That's the whole point," Avery chimed in. She and Kate had visited tables and added ribbons to their vests as well. "Cookie selling is about a lot more than just having fun. And it sure is a LOT of fun!"

"Yeah, one day I want to be an entrepreneur," Kate said. She firmly nodded her brunette head.

"An auntie manure? What is that?" Annie asked, scrunching her nose in disgust.

"An entre-pre-neur," Kate said slowly. "It's someone who starts their own business. Cookie selling has taught me some important lessons to help with that, like how to handle money and market a product."

Ella still felt uneasy about the job before her.

"Don't worry, my little sis, I'll be here to help you," Avery said. "We'll follow the five steps to success and you just might get a Cookie Activity Pin by the time we're done." She winked at Ella.